Of Forgotten Times

by Marisela Rizik

translated by
Isabel Z. Brown

CURBSTONE PRESS

FIRST EDITION, 2004
Translation copyright © 2004 by Isabel Z. Brown
Spanish publication: El Tiempo del Olvido, Taller, Dominican
   Republic, 1996.
ALL RIGHTS RESERVED

Printed in Canada on acid-free paper by Transcontinental / Best Book
Cover design: Susan Shapiro
Cover art: Diego Rivera, "The Well of Toledo" ("La fuente de Toledo").
  © Banco de Mexico Trust
Photo: © Schalkwijk / Art Resource, NY

NATIONAL ENDOWMENT FOR THE ARTS

Connecticut Commission on the Arts

This book was published with the support of the Connecticut Commission on the Arts, the National Endowment for the Arts, AND donations from many individuals. We are very grateful for all of their support.

Library of Congress Cataloging-in-Publication Data

Rizik, Marisela.
[Tiempo del olvido. English]
Of forgotten times / by Marisela Rizik ; translated by Isabel Z.
Brown.— 1st ed.
p. cm.
ISBN 1-931896-00-3 (pbk. : alk. paper)
I. Brown, Isabel Zakrzewski. II. Title.
PQ7409.2.R56T5413 2003
863'.64—dc22
                                  2003018082

published by
CURBSTONE PRESS   321 Jackson Street   Willimantic CT 06226
        phone: 860-423-5110   e-mail: info@curbstone.org
                    http://www.curbstone.org

Dedicated to:

The two godmothers of this novel: Ylonka Nacidit-Perdomo and Isabel Z. Brown, for their undaunted faith in this book since the moment they first read it.

And to John F. Graham, who kept reminding me about my passion for writing.

OF FORGOTTEN TIMES

CHAPTER 1

Enraged, Facundo Miranda paced the room like a caged animal. He could have any woman he wanted. But *that* one, the protégé of the former slaves, the only one who could satisfy his hunger, he couldn't have. He could force her to be his, but he rejected that option. Not because he lacked the capacity to do so but because he deeply feared the magic of those who protected her. Facundo Miranda had always gotten his way, and this unfamiliar feeling of helplessness infuriated him. His internal struggle would always end with the same muttered threat: "Like it or not you're going to be mine." Then, like a frightened child, he would steal away into a corner and pinch himself all over to extinguish the passion that consumed him. Convulsed by the sheer force of his obsession, he would ultimately surrender in this all out-war against himself. Eventually coming to, he would clean himself briskly. Embarrassed, his macho pride wounded, he would put his cowboy hat back on, and be back in control.

It was the beginning of the twentieth century. In the town of La Costa, Facundo Miranda finally found the solitude he had pursued all his life. In exile from another continent, he arrived and took possession of the land before him, just like the *conquistadores* who had preceded him long before. He planted a cross, put up a fence, and signed an imaginary document by which he declared himself sole proprietor.

Facundo Miranda had chosen this particular area, not by chance but by tracing the path to the lost town of La Costa as described in Father Emanuel Alvarez's diary, at least four centuries earlier. No one had actually seen or read Father Emanuel's original diary for a long time because the Church had confiscated the manuscript immediately after the prelate's death, storing it in a hidden urn catalogued under the title "Lost Lamb." How, then, had Father Emanuel Alvarez's forbidden secret become public? Various theories were posited. One, for example, was that the Church initially ignored the embarrassing and compromising descriptions made by the priest and did not address the issue with the urgency it indeed merited. This lapse in judgment allowed for the contents of the diary to be read by many. Eventually, despite the Church's censorship, the stories about the mystical village of La Costa, inhabited by former slaves and green-eyed women, made their way into the popular imagination. According to one of the versions, Father Emanuel Alvarez was an unrivaled expert at converting the unfaithful, by hook or by crook. Unstoppable and driven by his proselytizing mission, he was on his way to the inhospitable coastal regions of this country when he lost his guide. Almost dead, he was rescued by a peculiar tribe made up of former slaves. In his diary he described the green-eyed woman who lived among the slaves, the uses of exotic hallucinogenic plants with which the slaves controlled him, and their bewitching rituals. He also wrote about how the green-eyed woman seduced him. Father Emanuel was found blindfolded, near the village from which he had set out many years before, unequivocally assured that God was with him. He spent the rest of his life on the verge of insanity because no one believed his story. Finally, persecuted by hallucinations, he died. The tragedy for the Church was not that it had lost one of its most ardent adherents, but that Father Emanuel Alvarez had begun denouncing celibacy, pointing out that it went against human nature. In the middle of Mass he would loudly proclaim that the whole concept of abstinence was no more than an ingenious ploy, engineered by the Church, to ensure control over its parishioners. Be that as it may, the fact is that throughout time, many journeyed in pursuit of the legend, adding new details to the story that are too incredible to mention here.

The advent of the twentieth century brought progress. New roads made it possible to reach the isolated villages dotting the coast. Along with progress came the souvenir hawkers who, hearing about the legend of Father Emanuel Alvarez, saw an opportunity to create a consumer demand. They searched out all the green-eyed women they could find and sent them off with papers that certified them as descendants of the green-eyed woman described in Father Emanuel Alvarez's diary. By the time of Facundo Miranda's arrival, the people of La Costa supported themselves entirely by means of this legend.

Facundo Miranda was crossing the area known in the village as "Slave Hill," when he saw Lorenza Parduz for the first time. He was surprised to see that she ignored him completely, for he took it for granted that all of the green-eyed women in La Costa were for sale. Provoked and intrigued by her indifference, he followed her. He discovered that she lived on the outskirts of town, among the descendants of the former slaves who centuries before had escaped the horrors of the sugarcane plantations. These people had completely resisted the modernizing changes that had taken place in town. Facundo Miranda then inquired about the inhabitants of this village and was told that it was governed by The Council of Twelve. The Council was made up of men and women and a witch doctor named Taní.

Facundo discovered that nothing was done without the approval of The Council, which, in turn, consulted the spirits. When he questioned the inhabitants of the village about the young, green-eyed woman, they explained to him, as if it were the most natural thing in the world, that she was the last descendant of the first Parduz who had lived among the founding fathers of La Costa. They then related various versions of the origin of the first Parduz. One of the versions was that she had been abandoned on the beach by pirates, who had kidnapped her from her native land, and that the slaves, guided by spirits, had rescued and protected her. Facundo Miranda tried to find out more, but all he heard was a nostalgic lament whereby the villagers assured him that before the arrival of progress and the legend of Father Emanuel, the village had been a quiet place, where no one lacked anything. Facundo then tried to make sense of the oral history of the village and in this way discover the true origin of Lorenza Parduz, but to no avail. When he pressured the villagers, pointing out the many contradictions in what they told him, they would shrug and say, "This is what we have always been told." The conversation would then come to an abrupt end because the truth Facundo Miranda demanded to know meant nothing to the village people. Whether it was true or not, the mere possibility that Lorenza might be a direct descendant of the legendary woman described in Father Emanuel Alvarez's diary, fueled Facundo Miranda's desire. She was going to be his, no matter what the cost. He brought gifts and promised land to The Council, but they quickly let him know that Lorenza was not for sale like the rest of the women who were brought to the town.

Lorenza, who was sixteen, could not even bear to look at Facundo Miranda. Thoroughly repulsed, she rejected him outright. Not only was he excessively tall, thin, with a hollow face scarred by acne, but Lorenza was also fully aware of how he treated the women who passed through his life. It was as her mother had said, "At first they offer you everything and later, when they have you, they forget their promises and treat you like a slave." The more Lorenza rejected him, the more obsessed Facundo Miranda became. He was absolutely convinced that by the sheer power of his wealth Lorenza would one day surrender and fall into his arms, no longer able to resist his charms.

Facundo Miranda was not to realize his fantasies, for Lorenza Parduz's life took a detour which would carry her far from the town of La Costa. It happened one day when a stranger approached her, identifying himself as her father.

"You're being taught to worship the devil. I want to save you because you are my daughter," said the stranger, whose name was Maldonado.

The man's words stopped her in her tracks. She studied him carefully. He was thin, with sunken cheeks, and had a cross hanging from his neck. Her mother had told her that during her initiation ceremony she would learn the truth about her father, along with all the secrets that she needed to pass on to the next generation of Parduz. Lorenza was about to continue on her way when she saw the man fall to his knees. He begged her to listen to him for just a moment, that was all. Moved by what she saw, she stood still. The man spoke to her of a heaven she had never heard of, and of a devil who burned people like her mother, and of The Council of Twelve who, according to the man, worshiped him. He spoke of the years that he had spent trying to reach her and how his quest had been blocked by the devil and The Council. But he had never abandoned the search and was now prepared to do anything because God was on his side. Maldonado realized that Lorenza did not seem to be swayed by what he was telling her, so he changed his tactics. He asked her if she didn't find it strange that The Council would not allow her to leave the village like the other girls her age. This question and others like it opened a door that Lorenza, by herself, would never have opened because she had been brought up to respect the elders and their traditions totally and unequivocally. Now thoughts came to her which she never before would have dared admit to herself: that she actually was curious about the girls from the nearby village with whom she was not allowed to be friendly and that she was tired of the ancestral ceremony involving her mother and The Council. Lorenza and Maldonado agreed to meet the next day, near the well where she frequently went to get water. It didn't take long for Maldonado to convince Lorenza that his world was better than the one she knew.

"Lorenza, you have altered your destiny."

That was the only thing her mother said. She didn't try to change Lorenza's mind although The Council did, albeit in vain. Lorenza announced that she was going to convert to her father's religion. As a result, and by order of The Council of Twelve, the members of the village were forbidden to speak to her. Maldonado convinced Lorenza to leave with him and she went, thinking that by going she would punish her mother's and The Council's silence.

CHAPTER 2

Maldonado was indeed Lorenza's father. As a youth he had been handsome and good-natured. Because of this, and for other reasons, he was chosen by Rolanda Parduz to conceive her daughter. Rolanda Parduz exercised many important roles within The Council. She interpreted dreams and studied the phases of the moon to determine when to plant rice and fruit. Traditionally, the Parduz women would select the man that would father their daughters from dreams. The relationship with the chosen man would be brief. Instead, the interpreter of dreams would devote all of her energy and concentration to the new life in her womb. As soon as the witch doctor Taní confirmed a pregnancy, the man would be dispatched with gifts and banned from the area. Maldonado, however, had been a problem from the start. First, he broke the initial agreement and tore off his blindfold in the presence of Rolanda Parduz. The blindfolding procedure was meant to keep men from falling in love with the woman they were impregnating, because in the past, many men had wanted to return to the village. Maldonado did not honor the second or the third agreement either. The second forbade him from ever returning to the village, and the third required him to renounce all paternal claims.

Lorenza was born with her eyes open. Rolanda immediately realized that an error had been made in how she interpreted her dreams and that she had chosen the wrong man. That is why she did not try to stop Lorenza when she decided to go off with her father. She felt that, to a degree, the mistake had been hers. It is said that from then on Rolanda lost confidence in her abilities. She shut herself up in her hut and little by little ceased to eat. When The Council of Twelve tried to console her, she tearfully responded, "If only I didn't have the ability to see the future, if only I could rip out that which I can see beyond my eyes. Others are going to pay for my mistake." The grief killed her.

CHAPTER 3

Lorenza learned of her mother's death from a dream. She begged her father to let her return to La Costa but, enraged by the mere suggestion, he denied her request. For him, believing one's dreams was simply superstition, which reminded him of the forbidden rituals of the village. He locked Lorenza up in her room and ordered her to pray to God asking Him to purge her of all evil. He gave her nothing to eat for three days and made her swear she would forsake all that which, for him, was no more than devil worship. Lorenza cried bitterly and asked herself why her mother, who could see the future, had not saved her from this fate. On the isolated farm where she now lived with her father, Lorenza had no choice but to obey. Maldonado would not allow her a moment of rest. He made her sweep the dirt floor of the old hut where they lived until it shined. In fact, he jumped at any opportunity to mistreat her. The only time she saw another human being was Sunday at church. Her father never left her side, not even for a moment, forbidding her to make friends. He had long since forgotten the freedom he had promised her.

One night, Maldonado had a toothache. He sent Lorenza to borrow aspirin from the neighbor. Lorenza, who had always been afraid of the dark, pleaded with him to wait until the following morning because the neighbor's house was far away. This incited Maldonado's wrath, believing he had sacrificed so much for naught. Brutally pummeling Lorenza he yelled, "I saved you from the devil's claws and this is how you thank me." Lorenza didn't make a sound, which made him even angrier. He hit her again and again. Then he tied her hands and forced her to kneel down on a metal grater. He placed lighted candles all around her.

"We're going to remove that demon you still have inside you. You will learn to obey me once and for all."

The weight of her body on the grater's little metal holes made her knees bleed, but she didn't utter a word of complaint. Meanwhile, the toothache abruptly brought Maldonado back to his senses, and after some time had passed he repeated his request. Lorenza left, not daring to say anything. Once outside, lonely and afraid, she remembered Facundo Miranda, and all that he had offered her. It suddenly occurred to her that she might be able to get a message to him. She toyed with this idea for a while, but soon dismissed it, remembering that Parduz women never sold themselves. Arriving at her neighbor's door, she explained that her father had sent her for an aspirin for his toothache. The neighbor told Lorenza she had just taken the last one. She offered instead to send Maldonado a small amount of Chinese oil that she happened to have. Holding up the lamp to get a better look at Lorenza, she said, "You shouldn't allow him to treat you like that." Lorenza didn't reply. She thanked the woman and slipped away into the darkness. As she closed the door, the woman shook her head and muttered, "God gives children to the wrong people."

Amidst the darkness of the road the moon rose proudly and imposingly, lighting the way. Lorenza decided to play chase with the moon in order to dispel her fear of the dark. With her eyes fixed above, she imagined that every time she took a step the moon took one, too. This imaginary game made her feel less lonely and distracted her to the point that she no longer heard the crickets, much less the gallop of a horse drawing near. She barely had time to get off the horse's path. The rider cursed as he came to a sudden stop, startled to see anyone out so late at night. Lorenza felt the horse's labored breathing very close to her, and instinctively raised her arm to protect herself. She heard a man's voice asking, "What the hell is a girl like you doing out at this time of night?"

By the light of the moon Lorenza could make out the rider tugging at the reins of the nervous horse. She had never seen anything so beautiful in her life.

"I'm running an errand for my father."

"This is no time to be running errands."

"He has a toothache."

The stranger was about to continue on his way, but the girl somewhat intrigued him.

"I've never seen you around here before."

"I haven't lived here long."

Lorenza suddenly remembered her father—he would be furious she had been gone so long. Interrupting the man's questions she said briskly, "I have to get going."

Pedro Casals, didn't budge, blocking her way with his horse. He wasn't really in a mood to be nice, yet he thought it would be unkind to let her continue walking.

"Where do you live?" he asked her.

"Just beyond the Casals' estate," she answered, because that was how directions were given, using the names of the landowners who were known to everyone. Pedro Casals smiled amused, realizing that this girl was definitely not from around there.

"I'm going in that direction. I'll give you a ride."

Lorenza hesitated for just a moment. She had always wanted to ride one of those handsome sorrels. He reached out his hand to her and she mounted easily.

Pedro Casals was a landowner who lived in the city. From time to time he would come out to the country to check on the property he had inherited from his parents.

"What's your name?"

"Lorenza Parduz."

"And your father?"

"Maldonado Rodríguez."

"Ah," he responded, as if he knew him. And he knew him well, because Maldonado had worked for him before being overcome by his obsession for preaching to sinners. He didn't know Maldonado had children.

"Where did you live before?"

"In the town of La Costa."

Just thinking of the village where she was born made her cry. Pedro Casals pulled her closer to him. Lorenza could feel the stranger's heartbeat thumping on her back.

"What's wrong?" he asked, surprised.

Lorenza, embarrassed by her behavior, said quietly, "Nothing."

"There has to be a reason for those tears," Pedro Casals said tenderly. He pulled on the reins, stopped the horse, and dismounted.

"What would make such a pretty girl cry?" he said, gently caressing her hands. The man's soft warm touch made her forget why she was crying. Pedro Casals lifted her off the horse, all the while holding her closely. She looked at his face with its thick brows and eyes that she could barely see in the darkness. He tightened his arms around her and Lorenza, for a few moments, felt loved and protected. She was letting herself be carried away by the stranger's affections. Forgetting everything her mother taught her, Lorenza allowed herself to be seduced. Pedro Casals had assumed that Lorenza was just one more of the licentious girls from La Costa and was very surprised to discover she was a virgin. When Lorenza opened her eyes, she found herself on her back, on the ground, face to face with the moon. She thought that the moon must be waiting for her to continue her walk home, but she couldn't move because of the stranger's weight on her body. She lay there quietly, listening to the man's relaxed breathing, observing the darkened outline of the moon, which she had never noticed before. Without saying a word, as there was nothing to say, she pushed him off gently to one side, and sat up. She shook off dried leaves from her long skirt. He watched as she searched for telltale stains she could not see in the darkness of the night. He saw her shaking her skirt again and again and then smoothing it down, much as a cat cleans itself. Pedro Casals reached for Lorenza's breasts, which were now hidden under her blouse. He felt that having been the first man in her life gave him this right. Lorenza shuddered involuntarily upon feeling the stranger's hands on her breasts. Then she smiled politely and said quietly, "If I return now to my father's house he will kill me for being late. Take me to yours."

Pedro Casals knew by her tone and from the direct way in which she expressed herself that she was different from any girl he had been with before. His curiosity further aroused, he took her to spend the rest of the night with him. In the morning, he saw the dried blood on Lorenza's knees.

"From now on you belong to me. Your father has no right to continue to abuse you."

Maldonado swore he would kill his daughter when she didn't return that night. To appease him, Pedro Casals sent him money and one of his best cows. He wrote a note saying that Lorenza had given herself willingly to him and that she now belonged to him. Therefore, Maldonado did not have a basis for a claim. Lorenza, still fearing her father, begged Pedro Casals to take her somewhere else, far away. This was easy for Pedro Casals, and he set her up in a small house in another town, near other property he owned. He left her there with the promise that he would soon return. Sadness and loneliness were her only companions. Throughout the next year she lived as one more of Pedro Casals' many women. She learned that her new role was to wait and wait, and then to greet him happily.

CHAPTER 4

When Lorenza became pregnant, Pedro Casals lost interest in her. Desperate, she called forth what little pride she had left, sold everything and disappeared. She surfaced in La Costa where much had changed in just two years. After Rolanda Parduz's death, The Council of Twelve had lost most of its power because the younger members, following Lorenza's example, disobeyed the elders and ventured out into the world.

No one, except for Taní, came out to greet her when she entered the village. He confirmed that her mother's death had taken place just as she had dreamt it.

"You would have been successful here had you stayed," he said, sadly.

Lorenza wanted to remain in the village, but he said to her, "There is nothing for you here now. You can no longer take this path because it will lead you nowhere."

Lorenza left the next day.

"Remember," Taní said, "neither I nor you will die without seeing each other again."

They embraced and Lorenza left for a town very far from La Costa. She wanted to distance herself forever from her memories and her past.

CHAPTER 5

Lorenza settled in the little town of Santa María Redentora. There, with the help of a midwife, she gave birth to a baby girl whom she named Herminia. Impoverished and plagued by remorse and loneliness, she decided that her daughter would be better off if she lived with her father. She cried for days, knowing that this would be the ultimate betrayal to her mother's memory. Lorenza then took her daughter in a basket and placed it at Pedro Casals feet. "She's your daughter, and you know it. Take care of her, because I can't." This was all she said to the astonished Pedro Casals. She left abruptly, kicking at her horse while unleashing a flood of tears. Pedro Casals was reluctant and unhappy to be left with little Hermi. He sent some of his men to track down Lorenza Parduz, but they couldn't find a trace of her anywhere. Not knowing what else to do with the baby, he took her to his wife, Gertrudis Penn de Casals. She was a short woman whose face still betrayed traces of former beauty. Gertrudis had acquired the habit of eating to compensate for her husband's continuous infidelities. She deluded herself by attributing his lack of interest in her to her weight. Gertrudis had no reason to doubt her husband's explanation that the baby had been abandoned on one of his properties. They agreed to find her a home as soon as possible. Gertrudis then seized the moment to eloquently criticize the lack of self-control and the barbaric crudeness of common women. "Evil mothers, bringing children into this world only to desert them." In a calculated move, Gertrudis decided to keep Hermi and, just as she expected, all who knew her admired her devotion and good heart. Praise was very important to Gertrudis, and it more than made up for the sacrifice of raising another woman's child.

Lorenza reappeared a year later consumed by a gnawing remorse for having given away her daughter. She demanded her child back. This gave Pedro Casals the opportunity to unleash the rage he had been nursing for a year, and he yelled at her until he lost his voice. He hurled accusations at her, calling her "a wicked mother, a devil's whore, and an opportunist who preys on the rich." Laughingly, he scorned her for wanting to see her daughter. Lorenza stared him down arrogantly and remained silent. Pedro Casals threatened to turn his dogs on her if she didn't leave at once. In the end, Lorenza did leave because, deep down, she still felt that the world Pedro Casals could offer her daughter was better than her own.

CHAPTER 6

As little Hermi grew, her likeness to the Casals was undeniable. The first proof was her heavy eyebrows, identical to her father's and her paternal grandmother's. Then her mouth and amber-colored, protruding eyes like Pedro Casal's were additional confirmation of her heritage. And so the truth became unavoidably obvious, and Pedro Casals, although he tried to deny it at first, ended up confessing. Gertrudis suffered the worst humiliation of her entire life, and Hermi, barely two years old, fell into disgrace. Gertrudis' first reaction was to get rid of the source of her embarrassment as quickly as possible. She arranged a meeting with Pedro and his sister Florencia. Gertrudis was counting on Florencia's support to further humiliate her husband. Florencia was an expert on the genealogy, origin, and rank of every important family name in the country. It was she who alerted everyone when an impostor tried to pass for a legitimate member of an upper-class family. Her approval was sought out and respected, and those who passed the test were trained to pass judgment on others and to keep the circle closed. Pedro Casals, just to avoid his wife's and sister's reproachful harangues, was prepared to agree to whatever they decided regarding Hermi. Meanwhile, Florencia's maternal instincts got the better of her. After all, she had no hope of having children of her own. She was even able to overcome her deeply-rooted class pride despite the fact that she was mortified by the idea of her blood mixing with blood of unknown origin.

Florencia was transfixed by the tiny Hermi who was the very image of Florencia's deceased mother. Gertrudis, for her part, was flabbergasted to lose her ally. She angrily yelled that this was the end of the world, stamped her feet like a spoiled child, slammed the door, and left howling like a wounded animal. The decision had been made. Not only would Florencia take charge, but the child would carry the father's name as well. Once Florencia had made up her mind, Gertrudis' opinion lost all merit. Gertrudis swore that even though Hermi might indeed be recognized as Pedro Casals' daughter, she would see to it personally that Hermi would never enjoy the privileges of her own three children. That became her mission. For Pedro, on the other hand, his sister's decision relieved him of having the responsibility of turning his daughter over to be raised by another family. If his sister accepted the girl, the other important families would do the same without question. Gertrudis was left with no one upon whom she could discharge her fury. Tía Florencia protected Hermi from her sister-in-law, but she couldn't control Gertrudis' influence over her own children. As soon as Hermi was old enough to play with them, it was obvious where Gertrudis had sown the seeds of her hatred. She had trained her three children—Lorena, four years older than Hermi, Alfonso, five, and Laura, six—to never let Hermi forget who she was and where she came from. They took advantage of every opportunity to make her cry, reminding her that she was just a poor girl picked up from the streets. Tía Florencia couldn't muster the courage to scold her nieces and nephew, having always been soft on properly disciplining them. Thus, Gertrudis used her children as the ammunition she needed to avenge herself for all the things Hermi had supposedly, somehow, done to her.

CHAPTER 7

"I won't rest until you let her go, Pedro," Florencia pursued her brother with a Bible in one hand and a pencil in the other, poised to highlight a passage she was about to read to him. Tía Florencia had only recently immersed herself in religion. Through a revelation of sorts, she came to the conclusion that heaven would not approve of her brother's behavior. Saving her brother's soul from damnation became one of her many missions. Among other objectives she insisted that Hermi should get to know her mother despite this woman's dubious reputation. Pedro Casals finally relented, not because his sister's arguments had changed his mind, but out of sheer exhaustion from her tenacious insistence. Florencia did not doubt for a moment that a reward awaited her in heaven.

Hermi met her mother for the first time when she was seven. From then on, Florencia would send Hermi to visit her mother twice a year. Though the visits were short, no more than one night, Lorenza would spend six months planning each and every detail. Every time Hermi came, the people of Santa María Redentora would come out to see the little girl who always wore brightly crisp cotton dresses and whose face was concealed by a mass of black curls. The children of the town, stomachs swollen from parasites, would surround her and stare at her for hours, never blinking. Hermi would rock herself in a rocking chair, stubbornly refusing to speak, walk, or eat. Undeterred, Lorenza would narrate all the happenings in the village of the past six months to her little daughter. So as not to omit a single important event, Lorenza would record every detail in belabored third-grade penmanship. Thus, Hermi knew by heart that the town where her mother lived had once been very prosperous, but that the sea had carried it away. Lorenza recounted how once the sea had become very calm, and then, receded. The townspeople got up on their roofs to watch it. Then, in a flash, the waters came roaring back and took them all away. You could see all the little houses bobbing far out in the ocean while the people, still on their roofs, sang as the sea carried them away. On windy nights, one can still hear the mournful songs of those who had drowned standing on top of their houses.

    Hermi hated visiting her mother, and her silence was her way of protesting. Lorenza on the other hand, was overcome by profound sadness when the chauffeur would take Hermi away. After a few days she would begin preparing for the next visit, convinced that some day her daughter would show her some of the affection she so deeply desired.

CHAPTER 8

"Send her to live with the sisters," Florencia advised him. "Don't listen to your wife. She's a selfish, mean woman."

She was looking directly at her brother who avoided her eyes. Deathly ill, Florencia worried about Hermi's future and wanted to be assured that her brother would not let Hermi fall under Gertrudis' care again.

"You're going to get better...the doctors say..."

Impatient, Florencia interrupted him, "Oh, Pedro, I know you're saying this out of love, but don't make me waste energy on foolishness. I'm dying, and if you promise to do as I ask, I can die in peace."

Pedro Casals looked at her and couldn't hide his tears. Of the two, his sister had always been the strongest and the most determined. He didn't want her to die.

Florencia looked away, toward the wall. The pain that wracked her body was becoming unbearable.

"I'm going to do what you want, I promise," said Pedro Casals, making a concerted effort to appear to be in control.

Florencia released a moan that she had been trying to stifle for some time. Silently she prayed that God would come for her soon because the intensity of the pain didn't give her a moment's peace. At midnight, she asked for a priest so she could make her last confession. Florencia asked to be forgiven by all those whom she had at one time or another offended. She died at dawn. No doctor was able to explain what brought on Tía Florencia's sudden illness. Her friends whispered under their breath that her death was probably the result of an evil spell cast by a woman who years ago had sworn vengeance. This woman had been engaged to the oldest son of one of the most prominent families in the city. Although her mulatto origin had long since been watered down, Florencia unearthed it and deemed the woman unworthy. The groom was left with no alternative but to call off the wedding. Before witnesses, the mulatto, as they contemptuously called her, swore she would make Florencia pay for her disgrace. The cause of death on the medical certificate was listed as "unknown." But the rumor that Aunt Florencia had died from the effects of a curse that had been cast upon her persisted.

Hermi was nine when Aunt Florencia died. Since the school year had already begun, it was too late for her to be admitted to boarding school that year. Pedro Casals had no choice but to leave her at home with his wife. Hermi would never forget the eight months she lived with Gertrudis, for her every movement was criticized and the places in the house where she could sit or play were restricted. Her sisters physically abused her. Alfonso was the only one who stood up for her during this time. At first he too would remind her mercilessly of her origin, but little by little he began to take her side and openly criticized his mother's and sisters' spiteful treatment. Her other allies were the maids. Gertrudis would scornfully observe, "Look how well she gets along with the servants." Pedro Casals, for his part, kept his distance. His new mistress was taking up all his time. By not reproaching his wife, he could deflect attention from himself, and not give her a reason to start in again on the subject of his infidelities. And Gertrudis would not say anything as long as he didn't directly give her cause to do so. Pedro did not meddle in his wife's realm, and restrained himself from showing affection for Hermi, anything to keep Gertrudis from becoming jealous. Hermi, for her part, didn't question her father's treatment of her. But Pedro Casals did have to take a stand when Gertrudis decided that placing Hermi in a boarding school was a waste of money. "Leave her here where we can teach her to be a lady." Pedro Casals, remembering the promise he had made to his sister, enrolled Hermi in a Catholic boarding school. When he turned her over to the nuns, he felt that a heavy weight had been lifted off his shoulders.

CHAPTER 9

"Give him some time, he'll change," Gertrudis remarked to her husband who had grumbled that Alfonso showed no interest in anything he tried to teach him.

"Not the horses, not managing the business...nothing."

"He's only fifteen," she protested.

"Hell! At that age I was more respected than my father. Don't make excuses for him. There's something missing in that boy."

Pedro brooded. "What he needs," he muttered as Gertrudis was falling asleep, "is to have a woman. That's it," he thought triumphantly. "After he's been with a woman he'll give up all his odd habits."

Gertrudis had fallen asleep and didn't hear her husband's last comment.

Alfonso Casals, sullen and effeminate, was, from an early age, the black sheep of the family. The first sign of trouble was his habit of collecting butterflies. At first, his parents were enthusiastic about his ability to learn and to distinguish the different types of butterflies. Later, when he began to say he was communicating with them and decorated the entire house with their wings, his parents began what was known as, in the privacy of their bedroom, the Butterfly War. It was in vain, however, because Alfonso Casals was bound to follow his nature. And so, the more they forbade him, the more determined he became. Finally, his parents made a pact with him: he could collect and dissect butterflies only on weekends, provided there were no guests, and that the wings were only displayed on the walls of his bedroom. They thought that it was simply a matter of time. They were wrong. After the butterflies, came his obsession with reading, and later, his complete lack of interest in his father's business.

One afternoon, Pedro Casals took Alfonso out to the

country, stopping at a rural home, telling him that he had a surprise for him inside. Pedro Casals had previously made an arrangement with two young women. "Make a man of him," he had told them the day before. When they arrived, Pedro Casals excused himself under the pretence of checking on some property nearby, leaving his son with the young mulatto women. Without regard to any formalities they began to caress him, initially with their hands and then pressing their firm young breasts against him. Alfonso, recovering from the initial shock, found himself doing all he could to respond, but the exertion simply made his entire body tense up. The girls pulled out their entire bag of tricks, which had brought them success in the past, but nothing seemed to arouse the young Casals. The women's anxiety made Alfonso anxious, and at last he could take no more. Jumping from the chair where they had him trapped he ran out toward the hills. The women chased after him enthusiastically, laughing, believing that at last they had discovered a game which would lead them to their objective. But after chasing him for a while they gave up, exhausted. They explained their failure to Pedro Casals. Alfonso then returned, panting and embarrassed. He said good-bye, avoiding the women's' eyes. Pedro Casals remarked, in a cheerful tone, "The first time is always difficult."

Alfonso had not yet recuperated and simply stared at the ground. He wished he could disappear. Pedro Casals continued, ignoring his son's serious demeanor.

"My first time was very embarrassing. I was about your age," he laughed. "How time flies! I'll tell you what happened my first time. There were five of us, and we all went to a woman named Gloria. We had heard from the older boys that she was the best in town. Let me tell you. We saved for months to pay this Gloria, whose talents, as I told you, were supposed to be out of this world. We waited until each of us had enough to pay her because no one wanted to go alone. When we finally had the money, we went to her house. She showed us in without showing any surprise. What a beautiful woman! To make a long story short, she told us to sit down and asked our names, one by one, repeating it as she looked into our eyes. 'I'm going to begin calling you when I'm ready,' she said. Our legs were trembling, although we pretended to be in control. We waited sitting there as if we were in a doctor's waiting room. In a few minutes, she called the first name. We looked at each other and giggled because we couldn't believe we were finally there. Five minutes later, the second name was called. We were surprised because we had imagined that it would take somewhat longer. Gloria had another door for her customers to leave by, so we weren't able to find anything out from the others when they were through. I was the third. I went in, not knowing what to expect. When I saw her, I immediately understood what had happened to the others. I had never seen a naked woman before. Gloria had not even touched me when I exploded, and there I was, gaping at her like a fool. Smiling, Gloria said, 'If all my clients were like you and your friends, I'd be rich.' She held me for a little while, and there I was, finished in less than five minutes. Ah! And, as I got ready to leave, she gave me a coupon, saying that the next time I could come see her for half price. When we got together later, do you think anyone told the truth? Of course not! We all bragged about what we had done and seen. To this very day, I'm convinced that none of us actually managed to touch Gloria's body—at least not that day. But later," he patted Alfonso's shoulder affectionately, "later, I became a fighting cock. So don't worry, you'll see, the next time you won't be scared."

Alfonso smiled, encouraged by the story.

CHAPTER 10

Alfonso made a conscious effort to act according to his father's wishes. During his adolescence he became a party guy, sought out by all his friends. Pedro Casals liked the change and saw it as the beginning of Alfonso's manhood. When it was time to choose a career, he chose business administration because, in his father's opinion, it would help them manage their land holdings and investments. However, alone at night, Alfonso's doubts would almost suffocate him. Tired of pretending to be what he wasn't, he tried to kill himself. But he couldn't go through with it and decided to quit pretending. Pedro Casals threatened to disinherit him, but Alfonso knew that if he tried to live the way his father wanted him to, he would have to commit suicide. He asked his father to allow him to go to France for a year to find himself. Pedro Casals angrily denied him his request, saying that in his day all men knew their destiny from the time they were born.

CHAPTER II

"Didn't they come to pick you up?" asked Violeta, Hermi's roommate.

"No."

Violeta looked at her pitifully.

"That's the bad thing about being an orphan. You're easily forgotten," said Violeta, reminded of her own situation.

Upon hearing Violeta's words, Hermi could no longer hold back her tears and began to sob. Violeta lay down on her own bed and began to cry also.

With her bags all packed, Hermi waited all day for the car that would never arrive. Her brother Alfonso was leaving for France, and she had convinced herself that her father would send for her, considering it was such an important event. But the truth was that the Casals seldom thought of Hermi. Alfonso was the one who had visited her most often at the boarding school. He had promised to send a chauffeur to pick her up before he left. But Alfonso had lost all influence with his father, and his planned trip to France had been the last straw in their troubled relationship. He was leaving with some of the inheritance left to him by Tía Florencia because his father had refused to help him. Gertrudis, just to humor her son, had promised to send someone to pick Hermi up, but at the last moment found an excuse not to go through with it.

Hermi heard from her brother, months later, when a postcard arrived from the south of France. He promised to write her frequently. But Hermi didn't hear from him again until almost a year later. He said he didn't know when he would return. Over time, he had begun to enjoy the Bohemian life he discovered among his artist friends and he just stayed on. His parents heard rumors that he was living with a man.

After that Pedro Casals forbade that his son's name ever be mentioned in his home. "As far as I'm concerned he's dead," Pedro said to his wife, who secretly continued to write to her son.

CHAPTER 12

Hermi was deeply moved by the invitation to her cousin Raquel's wedding. Cousin Raquel was the only one who seemed to defy the invisible barrier Hermi's stepmother had created around Hermi. Gertrudis made sure that anyone who showed much interest in Hermi would pay for it one way or another; whether by having to endure a calculated indifference on the part of Gertrudis, or, by being banned from family gatherings.

Cousin Raquel, the daughter of one of Hermi's father's cousins, was ten years older than Hermi and had always showed special affection for her, in part because, since Tía Florencia's death, no one paid much attention to Hermi, including her father. Raquel was proud of the reputation she had for being intractable. So it didn't bother her in the least that Gertrudis had once remarked that she paid no attention to Laura and Lorena. In fact, Cousin Raquel instinctively favored Hermi over her two other cousins, and did so without apology. Gertrudis did not dare say anything when she learned that Raquel had sent for Hermi. Deep down she feared Raquel's rapier tongue. Hermi, timid as she was, never complained and behaved nicely toward her stepmother and half-sisters.

At the wedding reception Hermi entertained herself chatting with Doña Faustina, who knew all the gossip about those in attendance. Hermi noticed that everybody was looking at the entrance to the room.

"That's General Abelardo Gutiérrez," whispered Doña Faustina furtively.

Hermi had heard that name for the first time earlier that day, when her father happened to mention that General Gutiérrez was the new president's right-hand man. She had not paid much attention because, having spent most of her life in the boarding school, she knew little about what went on in the outside world. She looked at him again with increased interest because of how the other guests were reacting to him. She focused on details: the hair that was beginning to grey; the white uniform covered with medals. She looked away when a group, including her father, went over hurriedly to greet the new arrival and his entourage of four aides dressed in black. Hermi had wanted to continue her conversation with Doña Faustina, but Doña Faustina was now directing her attention to another woman, closer to her in age and social standing. Hermi noticed the contemptuous glares that Doña Faustina and her friend cast toward the General. "Times have changed, Faustina. You have to treat everyone impartially so as not to get in trouble," Hermi overheard Doña Faustina's friend say in a quiet voice. Having lost Doña Faustina's attention, Hermi decided to go out on the terrace of the exclusive club where the reception was taking place. She felt pretty in her pink taffeta dress and very much seventeen years old. She went through the ballroom and walked out on the palm-shaded terrace where scattered groups of guests were chatting. Despite feeling happy, she also felt a bit lonely. Although Hermi despised the boarding school where she had lived since Tía Florencia's death, there, at least, the rules were clearly defined. In her father's high society world she felt like an impostor. It was a contradiction that she couldn't explain. On the one hand, she longed for her father's affection, for him to bring her back home on the weekends. But, when she did come home, her expectations turned into anguish, for she had to endure her half-sisters' and stepmother's mean-spirited insinuations. A waiter bearing a tray full of champagne glasses approached her. Hermi took one and swallowed it all, almost in one gulp. The waiter smiled at her with his eyes as she set the glass back on his tray. Then she decided to return to the living room hoping that, with any luck, there would be somebody there to chat with.

"Hermi?" She heard the somewhat unsteady voice behind her. Turning, she immediately recognized the young bearded man with glasses approaching. It was Antonio Figueroa, her brother Alfonso's best friend.

"Goodness! When did you grow up?" he exclaimed with genuine amazement.

Hermi smiled and shrugged in answer to the impossible question. Antonio Figueroa was a young lawyer with an impeccable reputation who made time to defend the defenseless. He looked her over carefully, trying to find the little girl he had occasionally seen when visiting the Casals. Antonio Figueroa's unabashed stare made Hermi become silent. Then he noticed her embarrassment.

"Well, what have you heard from your brother?"

Hermi's face lit up. Her brother Alfonso was very dear to her.

"He said he was coming home for Christmas, but it's been a long time since anyone has heard from him. But you know what Alfonso is like, sir."

"Hermi, what is this 'sir' business? All this respect for me! You must really think I'm old."

Hermi smiled sheepishly not knowing what to say. The truth was she didn't know what to say. He continued, still looking her over, as she wrung her hands and her eyes shone.

"You know what? I've known you since you were this tall," he signalled her height with his hand.

Hermi searched in vain for something to say. So much attention from a man was overwhelming.

"No more 'sir,' agreed?"

Hermi smiled again, feeling her heart beating rapidly. Her flushed face and sincere display of shyness affected every fiber of Antonio's body. Passionate as he was in everything, he would have liked to kiss the lips that Hermi was unconsciously biting. Totally fascinated, he studied her for a few more seconds. She wasn't the prettiest girl he had ever seen, but she had a certain charm which illuminated her entire face, and her eyes betrayed a mysterious loneliness. Hermi raised her eyes and then quickly lowered them, avoiding his scrutiny.

"Come, let's sit down. I want to hear everything that's happened, including how it is that you grew up so quickly," he said lightly.

"Well, I can't really tell you that," answered Hermi, pleased to find something to say.

"Then we'll just blame it on Mother Nature, because you've become a very pretty young woman."

Hermi enjoyed Antonio Figueroa's flirtations and was happy to find someone to talk to. Moreover, she found Antonio very handsome. Aware that others were looking at them, Hermi was overcome by feelings of pride and embarrassment. After all, Figueroa was one of those sought-after bachelors. They had just sat down when a young man came over and greeted Antonio with a hug. Hermi was not able to see the look the men exchanged, but she did notice the change of expression in Antonio's eyes. Figueroa tried to smile as he directed his attention back to Hermi, but the intensity was gone. His eyes were inexpressive, almost lifeless.

"There are a few things Diego and I have to discuss ...business matters, boring stuff. I'm leaving you now solely on the condition that we'll finish this conversation at some other time. Will you promise me that?"

He looked at her again, directly. She nodded, and in her eyes he read a promise that could not be communicated with words. As the men walked away Antonio's friend said in a hushed voice, "They've taken Mateo. Rumor has it that it was Iron Fist."

Hermi watched them go. Figueroa's attention had made her forget the hustle and bustle around her. Suddenly she became acutely aware of her loneliness. Pondering these feelings she entered the main room and looked around, vaguely hoping to catch another glimpse of Antonio Figueroa.

General Gutiérrez saw her enter the living room and watched her sit down next to a languishing blonde. From afar he could make out the dimples in her cheeks when she smiled. He excused himself from the newlyweds, giving Leopold, the groom, a warm embrace. Leopold was Don Manuel's son, a professor and lifetime supporter of the regime. The General walked over to Hermi, and, loudly asked, so everyone could hear, "Why is it that no one has introduced me to this lovely young lady?"

Hermi blushed, not from his words but from the sudden silence that overcame the room.

"Oh, please pardon me, General, this is my daughter Herminia," Pedro Casals introduced her with a nervous smile.

"You are a sight for sore eyes, Miss Herminia," the General said to the stunned Hermi, who barely managed a smile. He abruptly turned his back to her and disappeared amidst the men who were with him.

That night Hermi couldn't sleep, not because of the General's words, which had come across as mere social pleasantries, but because of the pride her father had shown when introducing her. As she finally drifted off, she could make out Figueroa's full lips, large white teeth, and black beard. Falling asleep she concluded it had been a happy evening.

CHAPTER 13

Mercedes slid the comb through her jet black hair and smiled into the mirror at her face, a face that reflected centuries of mixed races. In the upper corner of the mirror, she could see the image of her mother, ironing. Fascinated, she studied the distorted reflection with its shortened legs and elongated eyes. Turning abruptly, she found her mother doing what she always did—ironing other people's clothes. Mercedes felt guilty for her own happiness. What she wouldn't give to see her mother smile! She couldn't even remember the last time she had seen her mother happy. Luisa Valverde's face always bore an impenetrable mask.

"Mama, get ready to never wash or iron clothes again. We're going to find someone to do it for us," Mercedes said in an attempt to cheer her up.

Luisa continued ironing as though she hadn't heard.

Mercedes turned and began to put on her lipstick. "Well," she said into the mirror, "what do you think?"

"Seeing is believing," Luisa said without looking up from her ironing.

"You know what they say about that Simeón character. He's horrid and they say that no young girl is able to escape him. Anyway, what do you know about working for one of those jefes?...Who knows? Mark my words, everything in this world has a price. Nobody gives anything away without expecting something in return."

"Oh, Mama, you're so bitter!" Mercedes said.

"Don't you think I haven't learned a thing or two in this life?" her mother answered, and without another word, focused in again on the white shirt that would not take the iron.

"I'm late," Mercedes said.

Planting a kiss on her mother's cheek, she left, thinking

that her mother always thought the worst of everybody. Mercedes hoped to prove her wrong, but she couldn't forget the glances Simeón had cast her way—looks that had caused her to lower her eyes.

When she arrived at the job interview, Mercedes was shown to a seat under a gigantic photograph of a general. She tried to get a smile out of the receptionist, a girl about her own age, but was ignored. She eyed the girl at the telephone with envy, noticing her long, well-manicured fingernails. They were painted bright red, and the girl used them to play with the telephone buttons with exaggerated elegance. Mercedes had unconsciously closed her fists, concealing her own nails, ragged from the daily laundry she and her mother took in. She resolved, from that moment on, to let her nails grow so that they would be just like the receptionist's.

Mercedes was beginning to lose the enthusiasm that had kept her awake for the past couple of nights. She wanted to leave, to run away, and to forget about the receptionist and her bright red fingernails. But then she recalled the guard who was watching the entrance. "What will he think if he sees me running out of here? That I've stolen something, in which case he'll chase me down and kill me." And she could see her blood-spattered body lying on the pavement and the guard quickly closing in. "Lord, save me from these thoughts!"

"You may go in now," the receptionist said, barely glancing at her. Mercedes instinctively walked toward the area where she had seen a door, a door which now opened suddenly from within. Before she could get a good look at the stony-faced cadet ushering her in, the door was shut again behind her. She stood with her back to it and wondered what to do. Looking around, she had the feeling of being in the biggest room she had ever seen. The huge room, with a high vaulted ceiling like those she had seen in some churches, was very different from the waiting area, Lamps were suspended from the ceiling in two perfect rows. At the very end of the room, where the last two lamps ended, sat a man,— General Abelardo Gutiérrez.

"Come closer, closer. Don't be afraid," the general said, taking off his reading glasses.

Mercedes stopped at the base of the stairs that rose up to the general's desk. There was not a picture on the wall, not a single plant, just the enormous desk on a platform at the top of the steps that reached the platform in front, in back, and on both sides.

"Sit down."

Mercedes sat in the only chair, by the stairs. The general asked about her age, her work experience, whether she had a boyfriend, and other questions Mercedes later tried to remember but couldn't. Couldn't because the look in the general's eyes paralyzed her memory, and the noise her heart was making kept her from concentrating. She came to her senses when she felt the general's cold hands caress her adolescent breasts. She could see herself sitting motionless on the purple velvet chair with her hands in her lap, waiting in silence as she had waited years ago, when a neighbor had dragged her to his room, covering her mouth to prevent her from screaming and keeping her there until he had spent himself inside her. After that, it was her grandfather, her stepfather's father, really, who would trap her in every corner of the house at an age when she hadn't even started to grow breasts. Later, he would bring sweets to pacify her, promising to bring more if she would behave. Mercedes had accepted her eighty-year-old grandfather's kisses as a natural part of her daily life. And when her stepfather left her mother, her grandfather had to go too. Then she missed him.

When the general laid her across his desk and studied her body with his fifty-year-old eyes, Mercedes didn't complain, nor did she feel embarrassed when he separated her legs and continued looking at her for an immeasurably long time.

CHAPTER 14

"Sweetheart, do you know how important it is that a man like General Gutiérrez has taken an interest in you?" her father asked, after Hermi had made herself comfortable in the chair before him. Pedro Casals played with a piece of paper he held in his hands while he tried to read his daughter's reaction. Hermi's face gave no indication of her feelings. He opted for saying what he had planned to say in case she objected.

"You're still young and you don't yet understand, but love will come with time. The important thing is to have a man that loves and cares for you. The general is the most important man in this country. It is an honor, you know."

He glanced quickly at Hermi but she averted her eyes. "The other news I have," he continued, "is that you will not have to go back to the boarding school."

Hermi felt the blood rushing to her head, and her heart felt as though it would jump right out of her chest. She could tell from his facial expression that he was waiting for her to say something.

"That's fine, whatever you say, Father. I will do what you say," she said with the sole purpose of easing the tension.

Pedro Casals smiled, pleased. The way children were today he had feared his daughter might protest what he himself considered to be an incredible opportunity. For the first time ever, he felt a kind of tenderness toward Hermi. He hugged her and she felt protected in his arms. Feeling somewhat remorseful, Pedro Casals gazed at her, seeing his own eyes reflected in hers. He knew that a marriage like this would provide him with great economic and political advantages. Life's ironies disturbed him; these advantages had come by way of the daughter on whom he had bestowed the least attention.

Gertrudis couldn't wait for her husband's conversation with Hermi to come to an end. As soon as Hermi left the room Gertrudis ran to meet up with her.

"My dearest Hermi, I know how bewildering this must all be for you. Poor baby!" She gave Hermi an affectionate hug. Hermi wasn't sure how to react. Her stepmother's display of fondness surprised her. Since learning of the general's interest in Hermi, Gertrudis had spent the worst nights of her life. It took a lot of effort but she finally convinced her husband to tell the general the truth about Hermi's origins. Pedro Casals was proud to report that the general was not at all put off by Hermi's history. Gertrudis' only recourse now was to win Hermi's affection. That morning she began her campaign.

"We must begin to prepare. The general called to say he wants to see you tonight. Imagine that! I've arranged for you to have the room Lorena had before she married. Laura is upset because she wants you to stay in her room, but it is better that you have your own room. I've asked your father for money so we can go shopping this afternoon. You have no idea how stingy he's getting. I had trouble convincing him that you need more clothes."

Hermi looked at the floor to hide her confusion. Then she got up and went into Lorena's room and remembered when her sisters wouldn't even allow her into their quarters. It had been a cruel game: first they would invite her in, but as soon as she stepped through the door they would kick her out. Hermi sat down on the bed. Tears began to fall. She hadn't even said good-bye to her friends at the boarding school, and she was unsure of her role in all that was happening. In the mirror, the image of a fragile, lost young woman stared back at her. Hermi fixed her eyes on the reflection seeking something within herself she couldn't find.

CHAPTER 15

"Why did I ever give birth to a girl? It's such a disgrace. I should have killed her so she wouldn't have to suffer...drowned her..." Luisa Valverde thought while tears fell furiously over the dress she was ironing. Mercedes silently studied her mother while folding her clothes and placing them into a suitcase, as if in slow-motion.

Luisa Valverde and her daughter had always communicated in silence. Anything that Luisa had to say, she said to herself. Mercedes hadn't told her mother what happened during the interview with the general and Luisa hadn't asked. Luisa Valverde had made every attempt to love her daughter since the moment of her birth, but she had actually never learned to love anybody. Her relationship with Mercedes had always been hostile. When her daughter was happy, Luisa felt it to be her duty to remind Mercedes of the misfortune and evil in the world. When Mercedes was sad, Luisa would hold her own life up as an example as she had never even known her parents and had grown up depending on charity. Mercedes feared her mother's silences and to compensate she often spoke for the two of them.

"Move in with me, Mama," she said when she felt that the morning's silence would drown her.

"Nobody loves me."

"I love you, Mama."

"And what good does your love do me? A son would have been much more useful. But you, just another slave like me..."

Her mother's words stung. She continued piling up the clothes without saying anything else. Simeón, the man who oversaw the general's private affairs, arrived at the small house Mercedes shared with her mother.

"Are we ready?" Simeón asked Mercedes, avoiding Luisa Valverde's eyes.

"Yes."

"Cheer up, you're going to live like a queen," he said in response to Mercedes' tears.

He took Mercedes' suitcase and turned to her mother. "You cheer up, too, Doña Luisa. Very few have this privilege. And besides, too much pride can be dangerous." Luisa didn't answer. Simeón removed an envelope from his pocket and placed it on the table.

"This is a little present so that you will not have to iron."

Mercedes watched her mother carefully, fearful of Luisa's defiance.

"Thank the general very much for his generosity," Luisa finally spoke.

"Consider it done, Doña Luisa, and anything else you need, we are here to help."

Mercedes approached her mother and kissed her on the cheek. Without looking up, Luisa said, "Take good care of yourself."

Mercedes followed Simeón out the door. She smiled at several of the neighbors standing at their doorsteps, bidding her a silent farewell. It was supposed to be a secret but everyone already knew her destiny. Some of them envied her; others only felt pity.

CHAPTER 16

"Everything is happening so quickly!" Hermi thought to herself while she was being fitted for her wedding gown. Again she felt like an outside observer to all that was happening to her. To her surprise, she found herself missing the hated boarding school and Mother Superior's frowning face. In her head she went over and over all that had happened since her cousin Raquel's wedding. For a full week after her return to school, Antonio Figueroa's intense gaze had invaded her dreams. Then came the official announcement that she was to marry General Gutiérrez, directly followed by all the attendant security measures that went along with her new status. She was alarmed when the general informed her she would need to get used to such precautions because there were many who would take revenge on him for upholding the law. What an incomprehensible mess it all was! And not a soul mentioned her mother: not her father, her sisters, or the general himself, as if she didn't exist. Hermi remembered her mother, the way she looked the first time she saw her: wrapped in a cloud of dust, running to meet her, while Hermi remained motionless and silent, struggling with the lump in her throat and a sadness that never left her.

"Perfect! A little tuck here and that's it," the seamstress said. "You can send for it early tomorrow morning."

Hermi came out of her reverie at the sound of the dressmaker's voice, which now continued. "Put a smile on that face," she said. "You should be happy with a man like that."

Hermi smiled blankly. "That's what everyone says, that I should be happy." She took off the dress and realized that the faster the wedding date approached, the more she remembered her brief conversation with Antonio Figueroa. His sudden disappearance, her stepmother had said, was due to his involvement in politics. Hermi would have wanted to know more about what had happened to Antonio, but didn't dare ask for fear that her questions would be misinterpreted. After all it was considered inappropriate for an engaged woman to display interest in another man. And even she felt that it was improper to be thinking of another man when she was about to get married. She repressed the memories telling herself that her lack of experience with men had made her believe in feelings that didn't really exist. After all, if the young attorney had really been interested in her, he would have found a way to say good-bye. And although at present she felt nothing for the general, "love would come later," her father had said. She was going to have her own home, and that was all that mattered. By the time she left the dressmaker, she was content.

CHAPTER 17

"Lucinda!" the general called from his office. "Bring me that article again."

Lucinda, the general's secretary for more than ten years, grabbed the newspaper clipping and rushed in with her pad and pencil. Her hands were moist with sweat as she faced her boss.

"Here it is, sir," she said in a muffled voice.

The general quickly scanned the three-paragraph article in the cultural section, which concluded with a brief biography of its author, architect Aquilino Ramírez.

"Have Rico Pérez prepare a report on that architect, all his connections, relatives… You know, the usual."

Lucinda was already on her way out the door when he called to her again.

"Tell Colonel Arriega I want to see him."

The general got up and began to pace his office. "Something always fouls up a perfectly good day." The oceanfront property he had found was the ideal location for his palace. He was planning to build it just like the sand castles he had created long ago on the beach in his home town far to the south. "And nobody—not that architect with his thesis on historical ruins, not any law—is going to stop me," he said to himself with satisfaction.

Lucinda was battling her inner demons. As a woman of the church and a good Catholic, she would tell herself she was only fulfilling her obligations. She tried at all costs to ignore the conversations she heard in the general's office and the names that appeared before her only to disappear into oblivion, later reappearing on clandestine lists of *desaparecidos*,—those who had disappeared. She would refuse to believe any of it, and when she could deny it no longer, she comforted herself saying, "Each soul will receive its just rewards in Heaven." Besides, she knew she owed everything she had to the general, including her house and her son's life. He had been involved in a student demonstration years before. If it hadn't been for the general, who knows what would have happened to him because few ever left the jails. So today like on other days, while inserting a page into her typewriter, she tried to forget her boss's unpredictable temper and the terror brought on by the general's request to investigate someone new.

Colonel Arriega, known to many as Iron Fist, stood before the general, who, in order to humiliate him, had not offered him a seat. The colonel was tall, with small, close-set and alert eyes that never stopped moving, and pointed ears that stuck out from his head.

The general observed him with a mocking expression. He deeply detested the colonel and despite his years of service didn't trust him. Little by little the general had brought Arriega to his knees: through humiliation, extortion, and by compromising him daily. But despite that, the general knew that Arriega was one of those who would sell himself to the highest bidder.

After a measured silence the general asked casually, "How are things going in the journalist's case?"

"Everything will be ready in the next couple of days."

"Good. Examples are necessary every once in a while. My position is difficult, as you know. Protecting the government, maintaining the peace. One has to protect peace at all costs. Do you follow me Arriega?"

"Yes, perfectly, General." Arriega tried to figure out where this conversation was headed.

"The sooner the better... And clean as always. I know I can count on you to do the job right. Have a good day and I expect to see you at my wedding."

"I'll be there."

Arriega saluted, drawing in his breath as he exited.

CHAPTER 18

Rómulo Palaciego always moved rapidly through whatever he did and had never feared anything in his life. When he met Augusta López, who later became his wife, he shrugged off his relatives' criticism. Why, they wondered, would a young journalist with a brilliant future marry a much older woman who already had two daughters? But he only cared about what he felt for Augusta, and any other practical consideration was an affront to his passion. So against all odds he married Augusta, who was ten years his senior, and now, five years later, it pleased him to tell the whole world that he still loved her as much as on the very first day. That's how he had always been, a pursuer of dreams. When others began to warn him of the dangers of finding fault with the military, Rómulo persisted in his outspoken criticisms. And if lately he had been a bit more discreet, it was not for fear of reprisal, but because his wife had threatened to leave him. Augusta was the only person left for him. His friends were keeping their distance and wouldn't return his calls.

"You don't know what it's like to hear the sirens in the middle of the night," Augusta would say to him, trying to reach him through his strong love for her. And Rómulo would reply quixotically, "Somebody has to say what no one dares to say." He understood the risks he was taking and was convinced that his international fame would safeguard him from any attempt on his life. So that morning he said goodbye to his wife and adopted daughters the way he always did. He was feeling better than ever. He had spent all night thinking about the editorial he would write introducing his theory regarding the country's administrative powers. He would declare that it was nothing more than a puppet government. The military, led by General Gutiérrez, was who truly governed. His wife instinctively kissed him once more and at that moment he seemed to look younger than before. This feeling renewed worry over the difference in their ages. Rómulo looked at her, pleased, but thought that she wouldn't be feeling so friendly when she discovered that he had broken his promise. He simply could not hold off any longer. The need to express his beliefs surpassed everything, including the love he felt for his wife.

Everything happened so suddenly that Rómulo barely saw the motorcycle carrying two armed men appear and disappear. He fell in a pool of blood, pointing with one arm toward the building from which he had dreamed of changing the world with his words. "There is so much to say!" he thought while blood flowed rapidly from the bullet holes in his body. The government sent condolences to his widow and relatives and promised to punish those responsible.

CHAPTER 19

Architect Aquilino Ramírez was not the kind of man who was easily discouraged. On the sheer strength of his own perseverance, he had built a career by selling lottery tickets on the street by day and attending the public university at night.

He had recently presented his final thesis in architecture, where he proposed the construction of a colonial district that would be, according to the conclusion of his thesis, "the pride of the entire nation." A bit cross-eyed, tall and slender, the architect had resolved to protect what was left of the ancient fort when he heard that General Gutiérrez was thinking of demolishing it to make room for the development of one of his own properties. For the architect the destruction of the ruins was a savage act, a deed that history would not pardon. Diligently he set out to prepare his case. He remembered his friend Paulino, who currently held an important position in the government. Paulino criticized Aquilino's preoccupation with an issue that nobody but he cared about. Aquilino retorted, "One day, someone will thank me." Despite growing up in the same impoverished neighborhood and knowing the same people, the two had never shared the same interests. For Paulino, Aquilino was impractical and idealistic, a man who would never amount to anything. "Just look at how persistently annoying he is toward the General over a historical place that no one gives a shit about! He's just asking to be thrown in jail," Paulino thought, while promising to put Aquilino in touch with a friend who was closer to the general.

When he was finally invited to see General Gutiérrez, Aquilino thought it was solely due to his friend Paulino's influence.

The general took off his glasses and greeted him as if he were an old friend, shaking his hand and inviting him to sit down, addressing him always by his title: Architect Ramírez. The general's friendly tone calmed Aquilino's nerves. He observed that the general was shorter and stouter than the papers and television made him look. He even dared to think that maybe the general was not as powerful as people said.

"So, you are concerned about one of my properties," the general began as soon as he had taken a seat.

Not knowing how to answer, Aquilino opted for opening his black briefcase and removing all the materials he had planned to show the general. He launched into his presentation, with the same confidence he exhibited when speaking of his architectonic dreams and visions to whomever would listen. The general, holding a pen between two fingers, paid close attention, occasionally scribbling something on a piece of paper that was in front of him. Aquilino continued his exposition, not in the least discouraged by the general's impassive countenance. When he finished, the general looked at the photographs of renovated sites in other countries. The governor's home from colonial times for example had been turned into a hotel. He liked it. Fixing his gaze on the architect, he smiled.

"You are a well-informed man. And I, my friend, appreciate well-informed people." The general rocked in his chair. "Come join my team… I want you to direct the plans so history is respected. What do you think?" the general asked as he stood up and approached the architect.

Aquilino was at a loss for words.

"Well..."

The general smiled, pleased.

Aquilino's thoughts were racing. Nothing seemed to fit. He had never been very interested in politics; but he was well aware of what everybody said about General Gutiérrez, including that he was directly responsible for the murder of members of the opposition and that, given the opportunity, he would sell his own mother's soul.

"You are not going to reject my offer, are you?" the

general asked rhetorically without waiting for an answer. "I expect you tomorrow so that we may begin."

The general, still enjoying the surprise he knew he had foisted on the architect added, "As you see, I am not as irrational as some people say."

Aquilino nodded without knowing exactly why.

The general continued, as if addressing an invisible audience.

"This country needs people like you. Look… I was about to commit an atrocity! Due to ignorance, pure ignorance, my friend. Don't forget, I expect you tomorrow!" the general concluded authoritatively.

He put his right hand on Aquilino's shoulder and led him to his secretary with the order to make him an appointment for the next day. Aquilino didn't have a chance to utter another word.

CHAPTER 20

Tears were silently covering everything: the pillows, the white sheets and what was left of the wedding dress. She could feel his breath—thick with alcohol and tobacco. She tried to control her sobs, but the knot in her throat was too much. Like a volcanic explosion emanating from the core of the earth, her sobs spread uncontrollably throughout the room. The general continued devouring her, indifferent, kissing her whole body with big, slobbery kisses.

No longer able to ignore the moaning that resounded throughout the room, he pulled away roughly, breathing hard and glared at her with bloodshot eyes.

"God damn it! Quit acting like a child! You are my wife not a spoiled little girl," the general was using a tone of voice that was new to Hermi.

Like a frightened child Hermi covered herself with the sheet. Looking at her the general was reminded of his own childhood. Rather than pity he felt rage.

"You can keep your screams," he muttered angrily, buttoning up his shirt.

CHAPTER 21

Mercedes was surprised to see him since she knew he had gotten married that day. She asked no questions, took off her nightgown and got under the mosquito net. He studied her for a bit and then turned his back toward her to sleep.

The nights the general spent with Mercedes were sleepless nights for her because she still remembered that night she had tried to strangle her cousin Martina while dreaming she was battling a snake. The idea she might unconsciously threaten the general's life kept Mercedes awake all night long. Those sleepless nights she arrived at conclusions about life that helped her survive the loneliness that plagued all the women whose lives crossed paths with the general's.

The general awoke at dawn exactly as the clock was striking five. This was when he usually left his mistresses' houses. He woke up to find Mercedes silently looking at him. It occurred to him that she had aged a lot in the three months since he had met her. It also struck him that he was becoming quite fond of her. Perhaps it was because she didn't talk all the time like the others. Mercedes remained still, contemplating the general's large veined hands as they passed over her body. She waited. He got up. Mercedes followed him in silence performing an act they had not rehearsed. Silently she passed him whatever he needed to shower and dress. Afterward, with his back turned to her, he placed some money on the night stand. Avoiding her look, he muttered the same words he always uttered, "If you need anything let Simeón know."

The general left. He saw his chauffeur and the plain-clothes men who surrounded Mercedes' house waiting for him...He then remembered he had gotten married the previous day.

CHAPTER 22

Doña Herminia, as she was called after her marriage, was surprised by the general's behavior. Until the night of the wedding he had been gallant and attentive. The glint in his angry eyes terrified her. She cried because she didn't understand what was going on and because she didn't know what to do. She cried over what her family would think if they knew that the general had not slept with her on their wedding night. She cried and kept crying, tormented by stories scrambled in her mind, of girls sent back to their families because they were not virgins. She saw the shame on her father's face. She continued crying over this imagined disgrace until she remembered she had no reason to worry; she had never been in another man's arms. As far back as she could remember she had been surrounded by nuns.

The only time she had fallen in love was when she was fifteen years old. It happened during Easter week on the day her cousin Juan Luis arrived for a visit. Juan Luis was a distant cousin; the son of one of her father's first cousins. Hermi knew of him only from letters because he still lived in the land that Hermi's grandparents had left long before Hermi was born. Don Rodrigo Casals and Dolores Almonte de Casals had arrived toward the beginning of the century with the intention of staying only for a short time. Given the intense heat and the preponderant mixture of races, the area did not meet their essential requirements. Hermi's grandparents, while poor, proudly claimed to be of noble ancestry. Their initial misgivings notwithstanding, they ended up staying, living on very little while they worked day and night. Over time they accumulated properties and established businesses that their two children, Pedro, named after his father, and Florencia, named after her mother, inherited. Don Rodrigo and Dolores advised their son to seek a wife in the land of his forefathers, to care for his older sister, and to find her a good husband. Florencia was told to always heed Pedro's counsel. Even though Florencia had many admirers, she never married. She dedicated the rest of her life to caring for her brother's children, especially Hermi—particularly at the time when she realized her suitors were no longer sending flowers or finding an excuse to visit her. By then she might have married any one of them, but all had lost interest.

Hermi discovered the power of communicating without words for the very first time when cousin Juan Luis came to visit. She and Juan Luis would seek out each other's gaze and, without expressly planning it, would run into each other in every corner of the house. Her heart stopped every time her cousin looked at her.

It was also at this time that Hermi realized that the solitary pleasure she had experienced by knotting up the sheets around her body could be a shared experience. Up till then it had been a game she had discovered by accident one boring afternoon. She kept it secret convinced that no other girls knew the private pleasure she had found between the sheets.

Each day Hermi sought out Juan Luis' longing gazes which would set her vibrating like the keys of the piano Sister Inés played at the boarding school.

At the end of Holy Week Juan Luis left for his homeland promising to write soon and to return that summer when he would have more time. But he never came back and the only letter he sent was addressed not to Hermi but to the whole family thanking them for their hospitality. In the years that followed he sent postcards from the various ports he visited after enrolling in the naval academy.

Her cousin, despite all his penetrating glances, never declared his love to Hermi. Perhaps out of fear or because he thought he would return, or because he just never got the chance. Who knows? Hermi, at times, began to think she had imagined the whole thing.

What she was certain of was the pain she felt.

The days back at the boarding school, after Juan Luis' departure, were tough. At any given moment Hermi would find herself distracted, transported to the days when her eyes sought her cousin's. Worried that someone might discover she was in love, Hermi lost her appetite. What would the Mother Superior think if she ever found out about the thoughts she couldn't control and for which she was ashamed? It was this shame that drove Hermi to confess her sins to the priest who came to say Mass on Sundays. Not missing any details, she described her thoughts from the time of her cousin's arrival to her return to the boarding school. When she halted at times, not knowing how to describe her feelings, the priest urged her to continue. Her penitence was three Hail Marys and one Our Father, along with prayers to God asking for forgiveness for "those bad thoughts." Despite her confession and her prayers, her cousin Juan Luis and his imaginary kisses pursued her for some time. Eventually the memories of her cousin began to fade until one fine day she found she no longer thought of him.

CHAPTER 23

Hermi awoke the morning following her wedding night certain that the general would beg her forgiveness for the brusque manner in which he had treated her the night before. The general ignored her that morning and the days that followed. The enormous house he had presented her with prior to the wedding now seemed small and stifling. She felt restricted in what she could and could not do. To make matters worse, she couldn't stand the sight of Simeón, the man assigned to protect her.

Feeling lost and lonely, Hermi hoped to die. The only friends she had were at the boarding school. She and her father had never been close, and her sisters had always ignored her. And her mother…the woman she detested and was ashamed of; even her presence made her uncomfortable. "Why didn't I die before I was born!" Desperate, she turned to her cousin Raquel. Raquel, like the rest of the Casals, was proud of Hermi's marriage; after all, she was the wife of the most powerful man in the country. Cousin Raquel would announce to anyone who would listen that the general had met Hermi at her own wedding…and it was only thanks to her that Hermi was even allowed to attend. Raquel also made sure that no one took the place she held in Hermi's heart. Because, after it became known that Hermi would be General Gutiérrez's wife, the Casals family suddenly became overly interested in Hermi and her future. Everybody would recall something they had done for her and for which she ought to be grateful. That was when Raquel pounced like a tiger on her prey, reminding everyone of their past indifference towards Hermi. So, when Hermi called Raquel saying she wanted to talk to her, her cousin let the rest of the family know, beyond any doubt, that Hermi had sent only for her.

Raquel delighted in the envy written all over Hermi's two sisters' faces.

Shyly, Hermi went over the details of what had happened on her wedding night. She explained that she hadn't spoken to the general, because she believed it was he who was in the wrong. Cousin Raquel exclaimed:

"My dear, I am so glad you called me!" She lowered her voice and moved closer to Hermi as if she feared someone might overhear.

"Listen, sweetheart, you're going about this all wrong," she said opening her eyes wide. "Not talking to him is a big mistake. Let's make a plan. The first thing is an attitude change—instead of walking around angry get yourself all dolled up. Act as if nothing happened. Ask him how his day was. Caress him lovingly."

Cousin Raquel noticed the surprised expression in Hermi's eyes.

"Darling," she said as she took Hermi's hand. "Take my advice. Look, your method has gotten you nowhere, right?"

Hermi agreed.

"Don't shut him out. If you want something don't demand it, simply ask for it gently, without putting him on the spot. You can get anything you want, but with men, you have to let them think they are in charge. Do you follow me?"

Hermi nodded.

"Wait for him tonight as if nothing has happened. And remember what I've told you," her cousin said, as she leaned back in the chair, satisfied with her own counsel. "You mustn't tell anyone else about this, because you know how people talk. You can count on me, I won't say anything to anyone."

CHAPTER 24

As soon as he saw Hermi enter the office he had in the house the general knew that his indifference had achieved the desired results. He watched her as she timidly approached. Without saying anything he walked to her and drew her to him, setting her upon his lap. He contemplated her, satisfied, congratulating himself on his selection of a wife. Hermi was not only a member of one of the aristocratic families of the country, she was also a simple village woman's daughter. He could use this information at any given moment to prove that he was a man who paid little attention to social classes. He smiled to himself as he recalled Pedro Casal's apologetic face as he confessed the truth about Hermi's mother. Definitely, in all this, he had come out the winner. Not to mention that his wife was also young and pretty. He kissed her eagerly, but remembered he had a date for a poker game with some friends. Hermi was feeling comfortable and even pleased with the general's caresses. After her conversation with cousin Raquel she had decided that her life was bound to the general and that she had no choice but to forget about everything else and to try to make him happy. The general told her he would be back that night. Hermi didn't ask any questions, nor did she bring up the honeymoon, which he had entirely forgotten.

CHAPTER 25

Hermi became pregnant during the first year of her marriage, and the general demanded she have an abortion.

"There are enough people in the world," he told a shocked Hermi. The general had vowed many years earlier to never have children.

That decision was made when José Abelardo, as the general was then called, was very young, a few years after the birth of his half-brothers, identical twins. When the twins were born, José Abelardo, who preferred to be called Abelardo because it sounded less common, was overcome with a feeling of jealousy that never entirely left him. He sincerely wished the twins dead either by hanging or by drowning. Abelardo would entertain himself imagining their drowned bodies floating in their identical porcelain bath tubs. His hatred for them knew no bounds. "Abelardo is a difficult child to understand," his maternal grandmother often said in defense of her only grandson whom she loved devotedly, overlooking his preponderant egotism. Abelardo rarely hid what he was feeling and would choose to reveal his thoughts at the most inappropriate moments. "I'll say what I think all the way to the Pope if that's what it takes," he would declare when someone reproached him for his lack of tact. No one in the family could forget the summer he visited his Aunt Elizabeth, his father's sister. Abelardo was about twelve. Aunt Elizabeth was known in the family for her unselfish character and her commitment to charity work. She never forgave Abelardo for calling her stingy and for accusing her of treating him like an orphan and feeding him her children's leftovers. Abelardo enjoyed the fear he instilled in his relatives, but he defended himself like a trapped animal if someone criticized his behavior. Only his grandmother Rosalía, with whom he lived from the time of his birth, merited some compassion from General Abelardo. His mother had died of a hemorrhage while giving birth to him. Rosalía steadfastly stood up for him despite secretly fearing him. "He is very loving when he wants to be," she would tell her children who thought that Abelardo should live with his father and stepmother. But Grandmother Rosalía, understanding her grandson's contradictory nature, knew that would never work. Besides, she felt it was her responsibility to care for the son of her dead daughter. Abelardo lived with his grandmother until she died. Years later, when he became General Abelardo Gutiérrez, he had a French sculptor build the largest mausoleum in the cemetery. "For my queen," was inscribed on his grandmother's tomb.

His father, an army colonel, loved his son but was put off by Abelardo's constant reproaches and his jealousy. Abelardo never forgave his father for favoring the twins. He kept his half-brothers at a distance for in his heart he blamed them for robbing him of his father's love. When his father died Abelardo locked himself up with the body for three days without letting his half-brothers see it. "…Because he was my father first and I was his son before you," he told them, ignoring their protests that he was their father, too. He denied them access to the funeral home and the funeral. The twins didn't dare insist as by then the general was already very powerful and many, including his half-brothers, feared him.

CHAPTER 26

Doña Herminia was undressing slowly, listening to the sound of the water filling the tub. She imagined he would test the temperature of the water with his foot and then get in floating and closing his eyes or perhaps play with the bubbling foam; then he would be at her side and she would wait until he turned his back to her. From the bath she heard his voice:

"I saw you talking all night to Miranda. She's a gossip-monger like the rest. Keep your distance from her..."

"She seemed quite nice to me," Hermi dared answer, while she slipped on a see-through negligee.

"You are young and naive and you know nothing about life or politics. What they want is to be your friend so they can get to me. They think they can trick you... Whatever they ask you, tell them you don't know. And then come tell me what they asked." Hermi did not say anything. She had learned quickly that with the general there was no use arguing.

It had seemed natural to make friends with the wives of the military men close to her husband. But as soon as the general saw her becoming close to any one of them he tried to separate them. It was a pattern she learned to quietly accept.

Life with the general was lonely. Contrary to what her family thought Hermi rarely attended any social events with her husband. Most of the time she stayed at home finding out about newly-arrived dignitaries and important events when she saw the general's photograph in the newspaper accompanying the president. At first, curious about her husband's reputed power in the country, she had asked him about his work and his relationship to the government. Her husband's answer was biting: "The less you know the better. Stick to being my wife and leave the rest to me." That was it. From then on Hermi found herself with her lips sealed.

CHAPTER 27

Mercedes was rereading the letter she had just received. It was from José, a childhood friend announcing he was back and wanted to see her. Mercedes wanted to see him, too, but feared the general who didn't like any strangers visiting her, much less men. She stared at all the objects surrounding her. She would gladly trade them all for her freedom. Not even her childhood girlfriends could visit her because, according to the general, she was above that now and no longer belonged in those circles. Her mother refused to live with her, warning that everything had a price in life and she wasn't willing to pay it. What good did it do to have all this wealth around her if she didn't have the freedom to enjoy it? She would have gone crazy if it hadn't been for María, the old woman who served as her housemaid, friend, and confidante. At first she had despised the old woman because Simeón had brought her for the sole purpose of watching her every move. Over time their mutual distrust waned and they were united by their loneliness. Now they took care of each other and protected each other from Simeón and the general. Mercedes thought she might love María more than her own mother and asked for her advice regarding José's letter.

"The only way to know is to take the risk. Go see him. One can't remain locked up forever, prisoner of this damned fear." María advised.

Mercedes couldn't believe María's words because it was María who, for all those years, had counseled prudence when Mercedes despaired. "He will find you wherever you go," María would say, actually protecting herself more than Mercedes, fully understanding she would be held responsible if Mercedes were to disappear. But the closer she came to death the less she feared life.

She read the surprise in Mercedes' eyes and, as if

speaking to herself, added, "Fear! A prison for the soul! If I had to do it all over I wouldn't be afraid of anything. Go see him. You haven't been as indispensable to the general lately, and should those miserable busybodies tell on you...make something up, lie, defend yourself."

Mercedes kissed María and stopped worrying. She picked up her embroidery, which was the only thing she had to do, and while stitching thought about how she had wound up in her current situation. She wondered what would have happened if Simeón hadn't been looking for a maid in the alley where she and her mother lived; if she hadn't been outside playing with her friends, he wouldn't have seen her; and if she hadn't been so poor, then, he wouldn't have seen her there; and if she hadn't bragged about her typing, then, Simeón wouldn't have offered her the stenographer's job. Mercedes went over and over the events that had occurred and how they might have happened, and would have happened, if they hadn't taken the course they did. She spent hours playing this endless mental game. She comforted herself thinking that her friends had it worse, but if that reasoning had helped her before it no longer did.

CHAPTER 28

Fulfilling General Gutiérrez's vision, the beach palace brought together the past and the present, because of architect Ramírez's influence. The architect had become both renowned in his field and the general's personal friend. The palace was built over the remains of a colonial fortress. Some structures, like the surrounding notched walls dotted with cannons, which in the past had protected the inhabitants from unwelcome visitors from the sea, were kept intact. Old stone columns and spiral staircases, and a small, deep dungeon, where in former times prisoners awaited death, were also saved from destruction and restored.

Doña Herminia met architect Ramírez on the day of the beach palace's grand opening. She was very curious about him for her husband had spoken favorably of him on many occasions, and that was unusual since the general rarely discussed his friends with her. Instead, at times, she would hear him bemoan the people's complete underestimation of the enormity of the sacrifices he had made on their behalf.

When she met the architect, Doña Herminia was taken aback because, compared to the general's other friends, the architect, slightly cross-eyed and shy, seemed an odd fellow. She had pictured him to be robust, talkative, persuasive. Herminia soon adapted to her new perception, having developed this skill as a means of coping with the events of her life. After meeting Ramírez she looked over the palace with her husband and assured him that everything was first-rate. She praised his taste. Giving him a kiss on the cheek, she told him she would be going outside to get a breath of fresh air. She greeted her husband's friends, who, apart from very special occasions, never brought their wives. On her way outside, she made sure that all was as the general had ordered. She sat on a folding chair and closed her eyes. The torrid air was making way for a gentle breeze. She could feel the sun warming her entire body. She was content. The sound of the sea beyond the walls relaxed her.

A voice behind her broke her peace.

"How are you?" she heard a man's voice.

Doña Herminia opened her eyes in surprise.

"Oh, Don Manuel. Fine, thank you. And how are you?"

"I'm doing very well. I'm really enjoying this beautiful day."

"Yes, it's very nice," agreed Doña Herminia. "Please, sit down."

"Oh no, thank you. I didn't mean to interrupt you."

"Don't worry, I was just killing time."

"Well, in that case I accept."

They asked each other about the family and the friends they had in common. Don Manuel's oldest son was married to Hermi's cousin Raquel. They talked about cousin Raquel who was expecting her third child. Doña Herminia felt the sharp pang she always experienced in her heart at the sound of the word "child" because she had lost all hope of ever becoming a mother. Her husband had sent her to work with orphans to rid her of her desire to have children. Don Manuel noted her distraction and guessed why; it was common knowledge that the general had no interest in being a father.

While they spoke Don Manuel scrutinized Doña Herminia, comparing her to the women the general kept for his pleasure. Doña Herminia was no better off than the others. Other thoughts plagued Don Manuel at that moment as well. For days now he had struggled over a message for Doña Herminia sent to him by a friend of his, but he was scared of the general who exercised control over everything around him. On the other hand, Don Manuel had a hunch the message he brought made him part of a special secret.

"I was out of the country recently and ran into an old friend," Don Manuel began. "He asked me to give you his regards…and he also says that he has not forgotten his promise to you…He said you would understand."

Hermi looked at Don Manuel with great interest but could not remember a single friend who lived abroad.

Don Manuel looked around to be sure nobody could overhear.

"Antonio Figueroa, the lawyer." "I don't know if you remember him."

Hermi pretended not to recognize the name. Don Manuel looked at her, disappointed. Summoning some strength he elucidated.

"He was a good friend of your brother Alfonso."

"Of course, now I remember. Can you believe my memory? How is he doing?" she asked, letting down her mask.

"Fine, but he misses his country."

"Why doesn't he come back?"

Doña Herminia's ignorance astounded Don Manuel.

"Well," he said, practically stuttering, "he is not allowed to return."

Hermi understood and was immediately embarrassed by her question.

"Yes, now I remember…something to do with politics…"

Don Manuel felt uneasy.

"I want to ask you a big favor, Doña Herminia…the situation in the country is rather difficult, and the general may not understand this conversation…You know him better than anybody. I would appreciate it if you would not mention this conversation. I ask you this based on the familial ties that bind us."

Doña Herminia understood Don Manuel's concern.

"Of course, don't give it another thought," she replied. "The general and I rarely discuss such things."

"Very good, thank you. And now, if you will excuse me, I am going to get a drink."

He moved away, thinking that only because of Figueroa's

insistence had he dared approach the general's wife. One more favor for Figueroa and then this uneasiness would come to an end. Don Manuel tossed down a shot of scotch and then coughed because he had drunk it too fast.

Hermi had forgotten Don Manuel's serious face and was remembering that brief conversation she had years before with Figueroa. Over time it had become more special, more colorful, with a lot of imaginary endings. She was flattered that he had sent her greetings. And of course she understood Don Manuel's fear; after all, the general worked for the government, the same government that would not let Figueroa enter the country. She considered mentioning the subject to her husband. If the general was in a good mood he always let her have what she wanted, and perhaps she could help the lawyer return home. But then she remembered her promise to Don Manuel and went back to picturing Antonio Figueroa with his black beard and broad smile.

CHAPTER 29

Architect Ramírez was one of the select few who over the years had never fallen out of grace with the general. Many of the general's early collaborators ended up in exile, in prison, or as silenced enemies. The fact that the architect and the general had maintained a friendship for so long was cause for debate among the general's aides. Nobody could understand why the general always defended the architect and treated him better than those who had helped bring him to power. Aquilino was aware of his privileged position with the general but could not explain it. Between the two there existed a sort of censorship that they each respected without ever having agreed to it. The general would tell the architect about problems in his daily life, his occasional anger with the men who served him, and even his domestic problems, but they avoided politics. The general became convinced that of all the men who surrounded him, the only one who truly appreciated him was architect Ramírez. For his part Aquilino rarely expressed his opinions. He was well aware that a moment of sheer camaraderie could instantly be transformed into agony just by having the general misinterpret a phrase. Little by little Aquilino had convinced himself that his conscience was clear: he wasn't robbing the government; he accepted no more from the general than was his due and he had no interest in politics. Despite the fact that Aquilino always insisted that the general only pay him for his work, the general would continuously bestow him with what he referred to as "bonuses for a job well-done." So it was that the architect lived as well-off as the general's other aides. Still the architect would always insist that what he had was just compensation for his work.

CHAPTER 30

Doña Herminia arrived at her father's house fearing the worst. The night before he had suffered a heart attack that, according to the attending doctor, was not a very serious one. It bothered Hermi that no one had notified her right when it happened. It was always the same, as if she didn't matter. Her father was sitting up chatting when she arrived. She gave him a kiss and then greeted her sisters. They, in turn, apologized for their neglect.

"We didn't want to bother you," Lorena explained.

"I am not dead," Pedro Casals said, trying to break the tension. "I'll be around for years." He couldn't ignore the problems that had always existed between Hermi and her sisters and felt responsible for not having done more to bring his family together. He loved Hermi, but found himself rejecting her because her mere presence reminded him of how unfair he had been to her. That is why, even though he wanted to hug her and tell her he loved her, he couldn't bring himself to do it. Their conversations were always brief. By contrast he felt comfortable with his other daughters and found it easy to joke around with them. Doña Herminia was hurt by all this. Her sisters and the stepmother, while outwardly appearing to have accepted her, never in reality stopped regarding her as Pedro Casal's bastard child. The sisters knew they had the upper hand when it came to their father and they used this to their advantage to get even with Hermi for the many times they had to humiliate themselves asking her for favors.

"Hermi, tell me. How are things going with the general? I haven't seen him in quite a while," Pedro Casals said making an effort to maintain an interesting conversation with his daughter.

"Well, I wouldn't know," Hermi confessed. "Lately he spends most of his time at the beach palace."

"Yes, I hear it's something to see. One of these days when I am strong enough to handle four hours on the road, I am going to see it."

"Hermi hasn't invited us," Laura said, annoyed that Hermi hadn't offered to take her to the palace which was generating so much talk. Hermi looked at her apologetically.

"Abelardo always has it full of government officials. As soon as I have a chance, consider yourself invited...Perhaps we can all go some weekend when he isn't so busy."

"Yes," Lorena exclaimed enthusiastically.

"We won't hold our breath," Laura said trying to force Hermi to settle on a more definite date.

"Don't be tiresome, Laura," Lorena said, feeling a bit ashamed of her sister's sarcastic tone of voice.

Pedro Casals tried to change the subject.

"Things are getting tough these days," he said as if talking to himself. "People aren't willing to work. All young people want to do today is to loaf around or stage protest marches... There's that nut, for example, who wants to nationalize half the country." He was referring to a small opposition party that was preparing for the next election. "That's something to be scared of. Now they want to take away what we have, and for what? To give it to those good-for-nothings."

CHAPTER 31

Don Manuel wiped away the sweat running off his forehead. Scared by the lonely road he wanted to turn around and run away. He then reproached himself for his lack of courage.

Don Manuel felt he was too old for adventures. He was bothered by the injustice pervading the country, and if at first he had supported the general he had grown to despise his overbearing character. But no one left the general's circle on their own account. That was a decision reserved for the general. So Don Manuel reluctantly continued accepting the general's invitations because the general became suspicious of anyone who refused him in any way. Everything had taken a strange turn since his meeting with Figueroa. Outside the country those in exile were waiting for the fall of the president and his supporters. Figueroa had put it clearly, "It would be better for you to be on our side, Don Manuel." He regretted visiting Figueroa, but had considered it his obligation to spend time with the son of the man who had been his great friend and sponsor. He had gone for that purpose only, expecting a social encounter, not a political discussion. Figueroa's ideas excited him but the truth was that Don Manuel just wanted to live quietly as a professor. He fully realized that the only reason he still held that position was because he had kept his mouth shut. "And who can blame a man for thinking of his family's safety above all else?" No, he definitely did not share either Antonio Figueroa's political beliefs nor his passion.

The man appeared; his face covered by a hood.

Don Manuel handed him the envelope.

"Thanks for your help. We'll be in touch."

Don Manuel was too nervous to say anything. He got into his car and left, while the man disappeared into the brush nearby. He was pleased with himself for having fulfilled both of his promises to Figueroa. Now, he thought, he could just relax and forget it all.

CHAPTER 32

Doña Herminia was pregnant again. This was the third time. She cried for days without stopping. Hating everything around her, she decided to end her life. She would do it in front of the general. Just imagining his reaction encouraged her. Finally she would do something he couldn't control. All morning she practiced pointing the pistol at her head. She would wait until he kicked off his socks and settled into his easy chair on the terrace by the pool. He would put on his slippers and reach for the pile of newspapers on the coffee table. Then she would come and give him a kiss on the forehead, keeping him company in silence. She would also reach for part of the newspaper. Then she would check on dinner. After dinner he would lock himself up in his office. Later he would go out for a game of poker with his friends. Perhaps he would spend the night with one of his lovers, returning at dawn, waking Hermi with his caresses. She would then wonder how the general could feel anything when she felt nothing.

"Today will be different," she announced to herself triumphantly. She would change it all. She looked at herself in the mirror: she, Herminia, the happy wife of General Gutiérrez who lacked nothing; the illegitimate daughter of the Spaniard Pedro Casals, was going to kill herself. She hid the pistol under the mattress.

When afternoon came she followed the general. But instead of sitting down as she usually did, she remained standing before him. The general heard his wife's voice and looked up to see her distorted image through his reading glasses. He removed his glasses. Hermi was pointing at her heart with one of his pistols.

"I'm pregnant and I am going to kill myself if you don't let me have the baby."

The general looked at her unmoved.

"Hell, what you need is a good whipping," he said with a coldness that caused her to lower the gun without realizing it. "Go ahead! Kill yourself! Then all I have to do is scrape you off the floor," he said, returning to his newspaper.

"It's you who should die, damn you!" Doña Herminia howled like an animal in pain. She aimed the pistol. The general threw his fist at her face with enough force to send both the gun and Doña Herminia rolling on the floor.

"Goddamn bitch!" he yelled, grabbing the pistol. "These are not toys for women!"

He yanked the sliding glass door that divided the house from the terrace so hard that he pulled it off its tracks and then locked himself up in his office until very late. Doña Herminia got up. Her jaw felt as if it were dislocated. She righted the plant the general had kicked over in his fury. Then she looked at herself in one of the living room mirrors as a darkening circle began to form around her right eye. She didn't cry anymore that day or during the week that followed. Hair in disarray Doña Herminia wandered about mutely. She didn't inspect every nook and cranny for dust as she had done every morning for the last ten years. She didn't attend Mass on Sunday nor did she visit the orphanage she was helping to support. When cousin Raquel phoned about coming to visit, Doña Herminia excused herself saying she had a cold. But she didn't cry helplessly as she had before. Instead she spent her time thinking and then thinking some more. Days passed and the bruise around her eye began to fade; her jaw seemed to fit together again. She had heard the general coming and going but they had not seen each other all week.

"I'm not suffering any more," she spoke to the bathroom mirror. For the first time she noticed two lines framing her mouth. "I am getting old and I don't even have children." Tears began to flow but she dried them quickly.

She confronted the general as soon as she heard him in his office. She told him, without mincing any words, that she would not have an abortion and that he could do whatever he wanted about it. If he wanted to kill her she could care less. The general ignored her.

The next day he left for the beach palace with the idea of spending a couple of weeks there to teach his wife a lesson.

The general's intention had been to be gone for only a short time but he had become increasingly absorbed by his new scheme at the palace. He was gone so long that there were few sightings of him in the city. He spent most of his time surrounded by hundreds of young girls gathered from various parts of the country. The older he became the more insatiable his need to see young bodies. The girls arrived daily from different parts of the country, attracted by promises of a better life. They were very young; some so young they had not yet begun to develop breasts. The general began by making a schedule for everything. He would wake the girls up at five and make them march around wearing nothing but military boots, a black tie, and a captain's hat. Then he would arrange them in rows. Sitting in his folding chair he would unzip his fly.

CHAPTER 33

The general came home twice during his wife's pregnancy. The first time was a Sunday during Mass. The second was late at night. That night Doña Herminia heard him and lay very still, alerted by his footsteps. She knew it was he because she heard him speaking with the two men who guarded the entrance to the house. She thought he would come in and beat her for disobeying him but he left half an hour later. She would remember it as the longest half-hour in her life. She never got back to sleep that night. At dawn she got up and found a note on the glass table written in the general's scrawl. "You have chosen your future." Doña Herminia repeated the phrase many times but could not find a logical explanation for it. She carried on, resigned. Some nights she would nervously chew her nails until her fingers bled, then she would remember she was prepared to die. That would calm her. The idea of dying provided her with unfamiliar strength, a sense of determination she had never felt before.

CHAPTER 34

Lorenza Parduz knew that the moment had arrived when she received the news that Hermi was pregnant. Despite her fear, she knew she had to return to her birthplace. It had been more than twenty-five years since she had crossed the country fleeing her memories. That journey had taken three days by horseback and boat. Nowadays there were bridges, and she calculated that with modern transportation it would take just a day to get there. From the car, at a distance, she could see women washing clothes in the river and half-naked children bathing. She remembered when bathing in the river had been her favorite pastime. The driver announced that they had arrived at the crossing. Lorenza got out. The closer she got, the more she wanted to arrive. She had never considered, not even for a moment, the possibility that Taní might be dead. "He will be very old but not dead," she told herself with the assurance that comes only from absolute faith. The town adjacent to her village had not changed much. She remembered the dust and the faded look of the people who walked about with their heads bowed against the intense sun keeping their heads bowed even when there was no sun. She saw women balancing buckets of water on their heads; that had not changed either. All of the images matched exactly those she remembered. She breathed in deeply and reminded herself that although everything still looked the same, it had to have changed. It was good that she prepared herself for a major change, because whereas the neighboring town was frozen in time, her town had undergone a major transformation. Nothing remained of the old town of La Costa. Lorenza opened her eyes wider and wider in an attempt to convince herself that this was the village she had left behind. She felt lost among the people who passed by her speaking a language she did not understand. She had to stop walking and look at everything again to assure herself that the driver had not left her in the wrong town. But then she knew she was in La Costa, because the sea was where she had left it. Nothing else was recognizable. There were paved streets where once there had been trees and thatched huts. Lorenza got her bearings by walking in the direction of the sea.

She knew that if she continued straight toward the sea, she would have to turn right and then, not very far ahead, she would find the place where the center of town had been. She hurried on without stopping. A skinny colorless dog followed her. A motorcycle crossed in front of her. "So much noise, such heat," she thought. She considered turning back but realized she could not give up now. Moving to the sidewalk to avoid careless drivers, she resolved to face whatever awaited her. She still had a long way to go before reaching the base of the mountain where she hoped to find Taní. Walking for some time she noticed the dog was still with her. She was sure that the dog was the spirit of someone she had once known come to keep her company. When she spoke to the dog, it wagged its tail, moving closer, content to find someone who would give it attention. It occurred to her that the dog could be Taní because Taní had the ability to turn himself into whatever he wanted. Lorenza stepped up her pace; she had to know soon if her old friend was still alive. Until that moment she had harbored no doubts, but the sudden specter of the sad dog made her pause. If Taní had died, then she had missed the opportunity to find the answers to the questions she had come to ask. She hoped against hope itself that he would be there just as he had promised years before. The further she got from the center of the village, the more she saw small huts like those she remembered. It was as if time had divided the village into those of the present and those of the past. Sweat covered her body. "I'm getting too old to be running around like this," she mumbled to herself. When she arrived at the old part of the village, she realized that at least there nothing had changed. Children were playing everywhere. She called out to one of them, "Little boy, come here, please." A child with torn pants came closer, looking directly into her eyes. "Do you know where Taní lives?" she asked.

The boy smiled mischievously.

"Ah, Taní the old witch doctor!... Of course!" he pointed the way.

"These children are so disrespectful! Witch doctor... But, my goodness! He is alive. I'm so happy!" She walked in the direction the child had pointed to. In front of a small wooden house where she remembered a palm hut had stood before, she saw a very dark, very emaciated old man. She slowly approached him, expecting him to run to her; but he didn't move. She faltered. He, sensing someone had arrived at his door, asked somewhat nervously, "Who's there?"

"It's me, Taní," Lorenza replied, awestruck.

The man's face lit up. He smiled so widely that his lips framed a deep cavern. He had no teeth. They gave each other a big hug.

"My, you're all filled out," he said, feeling Lorenza's plumpness. "My dear Lorenza, I have been waiting for you. I had to postpone my death until I saw you again."

Lorenza could no longer hold back her tears.

"Sit down. Cry all you want, that's what tears are for." He waited silently for Lorenza to regain control.

"Well," he continued, "tell me good news. I'm made aware of all the bad."

Lorenza looked into his empty eye sockets which were moving as if trying to see. He could tell that she was observing him and guessed her question. "A piece of coconut straw fell in one of my eyes and the infection ruined both eyes. Everybody thought I was going to die, but I knew that I couldn't die until I saw you again."

They laughed.

"I guess this means another Parduz girl is on the way," he said.

"Another girl?" Lorenza asked curiously. "You think it will be a girl?"

"Yes, of course."

Lorenza read sadness over his blind features. She attributed it to the memory of the past.

"In my joy at seeing you I have forgotten my manners. Give me that satchel you brought and let me put it inside."

"I'll help you."

Lorenza wanted to know more, but Taní's sudden mood change indicated that this was not the right moment to talk about it.

They entered Taní's house which consisted of only two rooms. Lorenza saw the altar adorned with statues of saints, lighted candles, flowers, and offerings Taní was presenting to the spirits.

Time had stopped in there. And, apart from lacking his eyes and his excessive thinness, the son of ancient slaves had not changed at all either.

"And who is still here?" Lorenza asked.

"Very few. You can count them on your fingers."

"Oh...everything seems so different!"

"Yes, at first glance, but on the inside, nothing has changed."

"And how are they?" Lorenza asked timidly.

"I thought you would never ask."

Lorenza shifted nervously. The reason she asked was because she knew Taní expected her to. She was doing it for him.

"Only two remain," Taní said. "You must see them."

"I can't..."

"Lorenza, that is your greatest fault...your pride. At times, misplaced pride."

Lorenza looked at him with the awe reserved for a sage.

"I know," she said, "but they made me suffer so much."

"And they also suffered. By leaving you took all their rights."

Lorenza recalled The Council of Twelve, those old men who for generation after generation had dictated the moral values of the settlement.

"Do you really believe everything could have continued the way it was going?"

Taní thought about it, trying to give an objective response.

"No," he finally said, "I think it had to happen the way it did, but we always resist change."

"They shamed me in front of the whole village."

"That was their last resort to force you to stay."

Lorenza was silent. She had always believed that they should have given her a second chance because she had been very young and did not know what she was doing. No...she would not forgive the humiliation she had suffered when the whole village stopped talking to her on their orders. The memories troubled her, and she struggled with her breathing. Taní changed the subject.

That night the ceremony began. Taní was before the altar smoking a cigar. He smoked parsimoniously as if he were counting every puff. Besides Taní there were two old men sitting one on each side of Taní. Lorenza and Frida, a woman dressed entirely in black, with eyes of a frightened owl, sat there also. They all waited in silence watching Taní from the corner of their eyes. He continued smoking. Suddenly, Taní cowered as if hiding from someone, then, he opened his arms in a festive greeting. Next he seemed angry.

"God damn it! Did you forget I have to have Cuban cigars?"

The voice from Taní's body was authoritative, very different from Taní's gentle monotone. Lorenza looked at the two men sitting beside Taní. They were Roque and Polimorfo, the only survivors of The Council of Twelve that had ruled the settlement way before the administrations of governors and mayors. Lorenza looked at them sadly. They were no longer the strong men of earlier times. She was thinking all this while the two men looked at each other to decide how to answer the voice from Taní's body. Roque, the one who looked the oldest, broke the silence.

"Well, Baron, things are tough around here."

Baron was the name of the cemetery's first inhabitant.

"You call me from so far away and offer me this shit? I'm not talking until I get a good cigar."

Taní's body shuddered and, as if awakening from a dream, he asked in his normal voice, "Who came?"

"The Baron of the cemetery," Polimorfo, who was sitting on his left, answered, "But he refuses to talk unless we bring him a Cuban cigar."

"Then we will have to find one." "If we don't he won't allow the others to come. We must please him," Taní said.

"Where can we find one at this hour?" Lorenza asked.

"Everything is closed by now," said the woman with eyes of a frightened owl. "You would have to go downtown and everything there is priced for tourists, very expensive."

"I will pay," Lorenza offered.

" Facundo smokes those cigars," Roque said.

"That old geezer is a spendthrift. He doesn't give anything away," Frida volunteered.

"Well we could offer to buy one from him," Polimorfo said.

"I'll go get it," Lorenza said, standing up.

"It is very late, Lorenza," Taní cautioned. "Take Roque with you."

"I was born here, and I know the way even if it has changed...Does he still live in the same place?"

"Yes, but he is a poor and ruined man," Polimorfo answered.

"Oh!" exclaimed Lorenza, surprised because Facundo Miranda had been one of the richest men in town.

The road that led to what had been Don Facundo Miranda's estate was lit by the moon. The house looked unkempt and the lawn overgrown. Lorenza recalled the orange trees that once presided over the immense property. She couldn't see them in the dark, but suspected that they too had aged. She was about to knock when the door suddenly opened before her. A girl, illuminated by the gas lamp she was holding, peered out at Lorenza curiously. Lorenza thought to herself that if anything was different about the village, it was that everyone had electricity, including Taní, who had always resisted all progress in the village.

"How badly off can Don Facundo be?" she wondered to herself.

Aloud she asked, "Is Don Facundo here?" to the girl who continued to observe her curiously.

The girl did not have time to answer.

"Who the hell wants to know?"

The girl waited in silence for Lorenza to answer.

"Facundo Miranda I am an old friend. I want to ask you a favor."

Don Facundo came out of one of the rooms that ran off the main hallway. He approached the entrance, trying to figure out whose familiar voice he had just heard. He moved with the aid of a walking stick which helped put his arthritic knees into motion. He stopped in front of Lorenza. She stared at him in astonishment. Don Facundo's face was a mass of wrinkles covering his eyes and mouth. Only the familiar aquiline nose protruded from the mess gravity had wrought over the years. Don Facundo tried to open the eyes that had once terrorized all who served him.

"Well, blessed be! You haven't changed, woman," he said.

Lorenza remembered that voice with its distinctive accent that betrayed that he was not originally from the area.

"And you gallant as always, Don Facundo."

"Hell! I still want to sleep with you."

Lorenza was quiet. Listening to him she realized that Don Facundo's soul hadn't changed.

"I have come to ask you a favor," she said, ignoring his comment.

"Well, have a seat."

"No, thank you. I'm in a hurry."

"Little Lorenza has not changed a bit. Always on the run. God bless! Time!" he said as if talking to himself, and added, "It must be because you were the only one who rejected me that I still think of you. Or maybe it is because of all those stories they tell of your family. I have yet to figure it out."

Lorenza tensed up, feeling the way she had at sixteen when Facundo Miranda offered her everything he owned just to sleep with her. The old man's perseverance and cockiness angered her. Don Facundo was as arrogant as ever. It pleased her to see him financially ruined and uglier than he had ever been.

"I would like to buy a Cuban cigar from you."

"Ah, trying to communicate with the dead again," he remarked with an ironic smirk that came across as a grimace lost in the mass of wrinkles. "I would give the little life I have left just to touch you. It's an obsession, I know."

"Don Facundo, please, the little girl is right here…"

"That girl is more woman than you!" he answered, enraged, feeling rejected once more.

Lorenza's eyes met the sad eyes of the girl who was seated on a bench nearby, apparently not listening.

Don Facundo turned his back, stretched out one arm while leaning on his walking stick with the other. Brushing away cobwebs from an old shelf he finally located the wooden box containing Cuban cigars.

"As you can see, I would still give anything for you. Only for you, and you alone, would I part with one of my cigars."

He held a cigar out to Lorenza and when she extended her hand he grabbed it. Lorenza felt the old man's strength on her wrist. Don Facundo pulled her close enough to graze her lips with his. Recovering from the shock she shoved him away in a blind fury mixed with fear.

"You'll never change, Don Facundo."

Don Facundo turned his back and began to walk into the main section of the house. The girl saw his humiliation and gazed at Lorenza approvingly. Don Facundo called her, but she ignored him, choosing instead to watch as Lorenza disappeared down the dark road. As she closed the door the image of her new heroine was still fresh in her mind.

Everyone looked expectantly at Lorenza when she walked in but her face bore no expression.

"So how did the old man behave?" Taní asked casually.

"As he always has," Lorenza replied.

She handed the cigar to Taní.

"How did he become poor?" she asked to no one in particular.

"Politics and cockfights," Roque answered.

"And his evil ways," added Frida.

Lorenza sat down while Polimorfo lit the cigar and handed it to Taní.

"The Baron didn't ask for rum?" Taní asked.

"No, just a Cuban cigar," Polimorfo answered.

"Well then let's begin," Taní said.

Lorenza was trying to forget the incident with Don Facundo. It was as if the control and self-confidence she had acquired since leaving the village had suddenly vanished.

"Now this is more like it," the Baron of the cemetery boomed. "To whom did you wish to speak?"

"Rolanda Parduz."

"That one is a wandering soul…"

"But how can that be, Baron? She died a normal death."

"Well, that is the truth. Something keeps her roaming the earth. Why don't you tell me what it is you want to know?

"With due respect, these are personal matters, Baron," Polimorfo said.

"Well, I know the answer and will tell it to you anyhow. The girl who is about to come into the world—it would be better if she were never born."

Lorenza twitched nervously.

"But why do you say that Baron?"

"Who speaks to me in such a tone?"

Roque signaled Lorenza to address him appropriately.

"Your Honor, Baron of the Cemetery, I am the interested party," Lorenza said. "The baby will be my granddaughter."

"She is better off remaining unborn. That is all I have to say...The cigar is about to go out and I have other matters to attend to."

"Here is a glass of your favorite rum," Roque offered. "And couldn't you give us just a little more information...?"

Baron threw back the rum in one gulp.

"What you have here are three generations of poor procreation. And now I will say no more ..."

"Baron, distinguished Baron, this is Polimorfo speaking to you," Polimorfo began. "If you find Rolanda Parduz, please tell her that her daughter was looking for her. This will please her."

Taní's body shivered. Lorenza appeared lost in thought.

"Were you able to speak to your mother?" he asked.

Lorenza, unable to say a word, shook her head.

"And about the child, what did he say?"

"Bad news also," Roque said.

"Sometimes he lies deliberately, " Frida said. "He's done that to me many times."

"Maybe that's what he's doing," Lorenza reasoned.

"The knowledge of the dead is not always exact," Taní said, trying to cheer Lorenza up.

"Roque, what do you make of his final words?" Polimorfo asked.

"I see offspring conceived not by the union of love but

by circumstances. There could also be accumulations of hatred and rancor passing from one generation to the next. Someone has to break the cycle. He paused as he searched for the right words. "Back then, this type of birth would not have been allowed, but these are different times, we no longer have power. There is nothing we can do."

"What fault is it of the child?" Lorenza protested.

"None. Just as we inherit our looks so do we inherit other things that cannot be seen."

Lorenza could listen no more. She wished she had never come and wanted only to forget everything she heard. But there it was—another cursed Parduz. Lorenza walked out of Taní's house. The night sky was brimming with stars and she gazed at them, fascinated by the twinkling lights glowing above her. For a few seconds she was able to forget her wrenching agony.

The men began to come out. Polimorfo placed something in her palm. She looked and found a small hand carved of jet.

"This is to protect the baby from the evil eye," he said.

They hugged and Lorenza realized, to her surprise, that she felt none of the rancor for Polimorfo she had harbored for so many years. Polimorfo looked at her and said, "We will help you in any way we can."

Lorenza looked back at him gratefully.

"This is an amulet to protect your grandchild on the paths that await her," Roque said to Lorenza as he embraced her. "You mother would be proud of you," he added as he departed.

The tears she had tried to hold back fell freely now. She had come, she now realized, to hear those very words.

The woman with owl's eyes watched Lorenza steadily and spoke without moving a single facial muscle.

"I have received word from other spirits that your daughter needs you. You must hurry...they've also asked me to tell you that the day you are ready to die you must tell your granddaughter this secret." She whispered something in Lorenza's ear that no one else could hear and then disappeared into the darkness before Lorenza could ask her another question. Taní was the last to come out.

"You must leave as soon as you can. That wasn't Frida's voice. It was the voice of one of the dead."

"Do you think she was telling me the truth?"

"Yes. Frida has good contacts," Taní answered. "She has gained the respect of many of the dead."

"But Taní, Hermi has never wanted me around her."

"It is time to set aside your pride. Hermi has wanted you near her for some time, but you have never given her a chance."

Lorenza was about to protest but Taní held up his hands.

"Go to her. Don't wait any longer."

Lorenza was crying. She had come here in search of so many things. And now all she felt was hopelessness.

"You've done well to come, Lorenza. But my father always told me that fever is not in the sheets but in the body. There," he said, pointing to her heart, "you will find what you are looking for. Not in these long-lost places that are only part of your memory...And now, let's rest, tomorrow you have a long day."

CHAPTER 35

Mercedes took advantage of the general's extended absence to enjoy a freedom she hadn't experienced since the day she went to his office looking for a job as a typist. The mere idea of going to see her friend José had her shaking for days because she knew that no one disobeyed the general's orders. Encouraged by the old woman who lived with her and using the pretext of visiting her mother, Mercedes went to meet José. Only a genuine curiosity to see him again was in her mind. She imagined that after they greeted each other José would tell her of his travels and adventures and then, after the visit had concluded, she would return to her usual routine. For his part José waited for her nervously, understanding the risk he was taking. But his entire life had been a risk from the time he was thirteen when he embarked with some friends to foreign lands in search of a better life. Since his return he had dreamt of seeing Mercedes. As soon as he could he looked her up in the poverty-stricken neighborhood where they had played as children. Luisa Valverde explained Mercedes' situation in a few words. Reading the rage in José's eyes she scolded him. "You have no right to judge her," she said, continuing to iron. After the shock of the news wore off José wrote Mercedes a formal letter.

What happened as a result of their reunion was an unpredictable surprise, something they had not planned at all. Upon seeing each other they uttered something like a greeting and hugged. The years of separation vanished. Neither could bear to pull apart for fear of being brought back to the present. Silently they resumed playing the games they had played when they were seven. He was the doctor and she the patient. The doctor would remove the patient's clothing one piece at a time to locate the source of the pain. The patient continued aching, silently begging the doctor to look further, deeper, her body screaming for the doctor's healing hands. And he, looking at the patient, would discover the same intense pain within himself. Eyes closed, their touches growing more intense by the moment, they did not know whether they were being controlled by childhood memories or reenacting them as terrified adults. Gradually, forgetting everything and becoming one, they thought they were the only people left in the world. Later, returning to the present, they saw themselves for what they were: two strangers at a complete loss for words. Neither daring to think what would come next. They said good-bye and made no promises. For Mercedes her accustomed unhappiness seemed more real than her newfound happiness. She had no doubt about which path to follow. José was devastated, his manhood destroyed, because now he had been with a woman who belonged to another man. José's brother, fearing for José's life, tried to convince him that sleeping with one of the general's mistresses was tantamount to a death sentence; but death to José was a farfetched idea. His brother then attempted to shatter his self-image by saying, "A decent woman would have killed herself first." His brother's words reached their target. José's infatuated heart began to spin in a tumult of doubts. He condemned Mercedes for being the worst of women. He hated her, for having seen her and for having remembered her all those years. He agonized, sleepless, trying to decide if she was a decent woman or a slut; guilty or innocent. He tortured himself for days trying to get rid of the numbing pain in his chest that kept him from thinking of anything but having her in his arms again. Finally, neither the jealousy of knowing her to be with another man, nor doubts about her morality, nor the danger he was subjecting himself to, could stand in the way of simply thinking of her. He wound up before her house and bribed the attending guard who allowed him to see Mercedes again. At first, because of fear, Mercedes refused him. The general terrified her, and she was scared of her own feelings, so different from any she had felt before. But she too was losing sleep thinking about José. Encouraged by the general's continued absence, she finally surrendered to a love whose intensity made her forget the danger.

CHAPTER 36

Mercedes continued risking her life. What she felt during her first encounter with love had helped her conquer her fears. But subsequent rendezvous with José ended in disappointment. When José touched her, she wanted the caresses to end, just as she felt when she was with the general. She couldn't understand what was happening to her because she thought about José all the time. The brief moments they shared were not long enough to love and to know each other. In the middle of their lovemaking Mercedes remained silent, fearful of interrupting José's passion.

Despairing, she confessed her secret to María. "When I'm not with him, I want him. But when he touches me, I want to run away."

"You're not used to being loved," María replied. "Give it some time."

With every encounter, Mercedes hoped something would change and that she would again feel the passion of the first time. But being together became unbearable until one day she realized that the only way to get through the moment was to return to her childhood fantasies when she and José had played at love without knowing it. She never revealed her secret to José for fear he would think she was strange.

CHAPTER 37

Pressured by international protests, the military regime supporting General Gutiérrez loosened its iron grip. Open elections were announced as proof to the international community that democracy did indeed exist in the country. Little by little a small opposition force gathered strength assisted by those in exile. After fifteen years of puppet presidents and military rule, people prepared for democratic elections. But General Gutiérrez and his men were not yet ready to relinquish their power, and that night they would make their final move.

The meeting took place in total secrecy on a navy ship. The gathering came to be known as "The Last Supper," because twelve of the general's closest advisors were present. General Gutiérrez told them, "We have to eliminate them before they take us down...you have no idea what will happen to you if these revolutionaries take over. Remember this when the gun in your hand shakes and your confidence falters."

He looked out the porthole and saw the sea that had turned dark like the night sky. His deputies were perspiring despite the air conditioning.

His back turned to the men, he said, "We don't have much time."

And then abruptly he changed the subject as if they already had all the information they needed.

CHAPTER 38

Mutely Doña Herminia listened to cousin Raquel's excited voice on the telephone. "Colonel Arriega was found this morning," she paused. "Murdered. Can you believe it?"

Hermi couldn't believe it. The news frightened her more than anything she had heard since the general left. She knew Colonel Arriega well because he was one of the few the general would see at any hour of the day. However, she felt no particular affection for Arriega nor for any of the general's close friends. Besides, the general had forbidden friendships with their wives. Hence her relationship with Arriega had been rather superficial. The only friend the general allowed Hermi was her cousin. Raquel had won him over with flattery, even though she sometimes privately criticized him. Cousin Raquel had the incredible ability to always get what she wanted.

Unrest was growing, and the political situation in the country seemed out of control. Hermi was worried about her daughter's safety and her own. After speaking to Cousin Raquel, Hermi went to check on her daughter. Little Sara was sleeping peacefully. Doña Herminia placed her ear upon the baby's heart to be sure she was breathing because she was obsessed with fear of losing the only thing she had. The letters she wrote to the general were never mailed. Finally, swallowing her pride, she wrote a letter asking for his forgiveness, knowing that he wanted her to submit to him. A few days later she received a note which read: "Do not leave the house until you receive further notice from me." Then, just to hurt her, he added in the margin of the note: "You couldn't even give me a son."

CHAPTER 39

Lorenza and the driver had given up on estimating how long the trip from Santa María Redentora to the capital would take. Under normal circumstances it would have taken about four hours. But that week beleaguered citizens had poured into the streets to protest the tyranny under which they had been ruled. The stench of burning tires permeated the air. Lorenza instinctively covered her nose with a little white handkerchief to avoid breathing the foul odor.

"This is a hell of a trip," said the driver, wiping away sweat that was streaming down his face.

Lorenza smiled in silent agreement. She was grateful to him for taking the risk of driving her to the capital. He in turn was pleased to have found a way to repay Lorenza for helping him with his ailing son many years ago. After seeing the conditions firsthand, Lorenza couldn't blame those who hadn't wanted to make this trip. Danger seemed to be lurking everywhere. A bullet fired by policemen toward the protesters could appear at the least expected moment. The July heat and the tension surrounding them induced long periods of silence between Lorenza and her companion. At the moment they were in line waiting to be searched. They had already been detained twice for this purpose. Lorenza assumed the police was seeking weapons. Once released, they resumed their journey. A group, carrying signs, was visible at a distance. They were demanding the release of all political prisoners.

"People aren't afraid of anything anymore," murmured the driver with suppressed glee. Lorenza didn't answer because she was buried in her own thoughts. She had always been satisfied with the miserly crumbs of attention that Hermi had thrown her way when she felt like it. And she, like a starving dog, had always been willing to lap them up without complaint.

CHAPTER 40

It was dusk when Lorenza Parduz and the driver arrived at the main gate to Doña Herminia's large mansion. Aiming their guns at the car's occupants, the two stationed guards approached the car.

"Get out," ordered the first guard at a distance while the other guard covered him.

Unrefined in her speech but sure of herself, Lorenza said:
"I am the mother of the general's wife."

The guard looked at her, then at the car, and finally at the driver.

"What's your name?"

"Lorenza Parduz."

"Wait one moment."

He signaled to the first guard and then disappeared behind the doors.

The maid knocked on the door to Hermi's room. Hermi had fallen asleep. It was seven o'clock and she assumed it was dinnertime.

"Doña Herminia," said the uniformed maid, "Jacinto says that a woman who claims to be your mother is here asking for you."

Hermi frowned.

"Who?"

"Jacinto says that your mother is here."

Hermi was unnerved as millions of possibilities swarmed in her mind.

She came out of her room.

"My mother?" She thought it over for a moment. "Go take a look at her and describe her to me."

The maid left and returned while Hermi waited convinced that it had to be a mistake.

"She's plump with long braids and greenish eyes."

"Tell Jacinto to let her come in."

Her heart beat wildly as she paced nervously in the foyer. Suddenly she felt there wasn't enough air in the house. She went out on the terrace by the pool fearing the worst.

Lorenza walked behind the uniformed maid. The floor tiles sparkled like mirrors and to Lorenza the house seemed enormous. The maid left them, smiling at Lorenza and looking curiously at Hermi's face. She had never heard Doña Herminia mention her mother.

Lorenza froze upon seeing Hermi. Hermi approached her and Lorenza was speechless. She took a few steps toward Hermi and hugged her. Hermi hugged her back and hearing her mother sob, without knowing why, she started to cry too.

"What has happened?" Hermi asked. She couldn't wait any longer to hear the purpose of her unusual visit.

Upon hearing Hermi's voice, Lorenza sighed deeply and said firmly, "Nothing has happened. I've come to meet my granddaughter."

Hermi looked at her without clearly understanding. She noted Lorenza's stout figure and the simple peasant skirt she wore. She felt the familiar embarrassment she had felt all of her life.

"Then come and see her. She's a beauty."

They both smiled, hiding the strangeness of the moment behind their smiles. Hermi felt guilty about never having invited her mother to visit her. It hadn't been intentional, but rather a mutually agreed upon decision that was never voiced.

They walked into Sara's room. Upon seeing her granddaughter, Lorenza was reminded of Taní's words and those of the spirits. She said a silent prayer.

CHAPTER 41

The general focused on taking care of something that had been bothering him for more than a week.

"Where do you have him?" he asked.

The secret agent gulped twice before answering, "As you ordered, we have him gagged in the car."

"And the other one?"

"She's in the house. She hasn't gone out all week."

"Does she suspect that I know?"

"I don't think so, sir."

"Well, follow me. We're going to take care of this matter once and for all."

The men walked to the black car. In the back seat lay a man who was bound and gagged. The general looked through the rearview mirror but couldn't make anything out because of the pitch darkness of the night.

"Let's go see the double-crosser," he told them.

Slowly the two cars and a jeep rolled off. The men, dressed as civilians, kept in radio contact with each other to ensure the road they crossed was safe. They arrived at the house located on the outskirts of town hidden among pine trees. The light was on inside. The guard at the entrance was new. The general did not return his military salute.

Mercedes woke up when she heard footsteps at her door. Her heart froze. She was about to get up when two men grabbed and pulled her out of her bed. The general stood before her. His eyes were like she had never seen them before: hardened, fossilized. Without saying a word, the general hit her with a blow that sent her flying into a corner. She felt relief instead of fear. The agony of waiting for the inevitable was finally over. He knew now, and she would be able to rest.

"Pick up that filthy whore."

Two of the men picked her up from the floor and forced her head back. Mercedes could feel something dripping from her face but couldn't tell whether it was blood or sweat. The general struck her again followed by two more blows. He grabbed her by the hair and made her turn in circles. He looked into her eyes and then threw her against the wall. Feeling something hard in her mouth, Mercedes instinctively spit it out along with some teeth. Blinded by the blows and the pain she was no longer able to think. She fainted.

"Bring cold water and bring the other scumbag."

One man brought water and the other dragged in the hooded man. They removed his hood, but he couldn't see because his eyes were swollen shut.

"So this is the son of a bitch who was sleeping with my woman," the general said stonily punching him in the stomach.

No sound came out of José's mouth.

"Strip him," he ordered as he kicked him.

José wanted to say something to Mercedes but couldn't utter a sound. They had been torturing him for hours and he could barely hold himself up.

"Throw water on the bitch and take off her robe. Let's see if they'll give us a demonstration of how they did it."

The cold water on her face forced her eyes open. Mercedes could no longer feel her body. She made out the general's spit-shined black shoes and remembered everything. She screamed when she saw José handcuffed, head bowed. She attempted to stand up but a kick sent her flying against the wall. Panicked and feeling helpless Mercedes began crying uncontrollably. She wanted to beg them not to kill him; she wanted to beg the general for forgiveness, but her sobbing overpowered her words. The general's men spread her legs apart and she felt José's blood-soaked body on top of her. Her high-pitched wails grew louder, penetrating every corner of the house.

"Shut the fucking bitch up," raged the general.

She felt another blow that made her swallow her last scream. José only moved his head in desperation. He could hear Mercedes' screams from far away. He wanted to move but his body would not respond. Finally he exhaled a painful moan. The general ordered his hands untied.

"Come on touch her or don't you want her anymore," he gnarled menacingly.

Placing his foot on José's back he pressed him against Mercedes' body.

"And you, you goddamn whore. Move it, move it...show us how you did it, you traitor."

José's weight on her chest suffocated her. They grabbed José's hand and made it caress Mercedes' nude body.

"This was my woman, you bastard. Take that so you learn not to fool around with another man's woman!" The general's last words coincided with a blow to the neck. He began falling slowly into a dark precipice. He could see himself in slow motion and knew that death was near.

"Get rid of them!" the general barked to the two men at his side.

He was leaving the room when the old woman, who served Mercedes, pounced on him with a crucifix in her hand.

"You will burn in hell!" she managed to yell before rolling to the ground from the impact of the general's blow, which had flicked her off like a fly.

"Filthy witch. Kill her!"

The general left the room quickly trying to conceal the way the old woman's sudden appearance had made him shake. The bodyguard aimed at the old woman. He felt an instant of hesitation because of her unnerving resemblance to his grandmother. Aiming his pistol at her he looked the other way. He never looked back and ran out as if something were pursuing him. Killing people didn't bother him but he had learned that for some inexplicable reason killing some people was harder than killing others. The bodyguard sat beside the driver in the jeep. In the back seat lay Mercedes' and José's bodies.

"Where do we take them?" asked the driver.

"To the old cemetery," answered the one who had shot the old woman.

The two drove in silence. They arrived, got out of the jeep, and took out the bodies.

"Should we shoot them once more just to be sure?" asked the driver.

"If you want to go ahead, but do it quickly because this place gives me the creeps."

The man looked at the two bodies and shrugged. He got back into the jeep.

"What's the matter?"

"They look pretty dead to me. Besides we have to ration the bullets...the way things are going we're going to need all of them."

They said nothing else to each other.

CHAPTER 42

It was about two o'clock in the morning when Dr. Armando Collado left the hospital where he occasionally donated his services. He was thinking that he was no longer up to those sleepless nights. Perhaps he should follow his wife's advice and continue with his private practice but forget about volunteering at the hospital. But he enjoyed feeling needed, and working at the hospital helped him remember why he had become a doctor in the first place. He was absorbed by these thoughts as he drove past the old cemetery where he passed by a parked jeep. He looked in his rear view mirror and saw two shadows leaving the cemetery in the dark. Dr. Collado tried telling himself that they were only drunks, but something in his mind suspected otherwise. Decomposed corpses had been found in the old cemetery many times. Fear of the dead frightened drunkards, he thought, but not assassins. He planned to keep going but couldn't rid himself of his curiosity. He turned at the first corner he reached, parked his car, and switched off the headlights. His heart was pounding. Suddenly he was wide awake. He waited patiently for ten minutes before slowly driving by the entrance to the graveyard. The jeep was gone. Leaving the car at a discreet distance he walked cautiously, figuring that if someone should question him he could simply say that he was having car trouble. The gate to the entrance of the cemetery was ajar. He detected two bodies only ten steps away. "They don't even bother to hide them anymore," he thought while running toward the bodies. He took their pulses. The man showed no sign of life but the woman's pulse was beating faintly. He threw the naked man's body aside and gently picked up the woman. He left her at the entrance to the graveyard and ran to his car. He had to restrain himself because, despite being athletic and strong, his racing heart reminded him that he was nearing fifty. He drove the woman to his private clinic and treated her injuries in the emergency room. He cared for her that night and continued to watch over her for several days, intrigued and moved by the tears that slowly rolled down her face. Dr. Collado knew that he should never get emotionally involved with his patients, but he couldn't help the joy he felt when he saw her return to life. He came to see her whenever he could. The nurse on duty, noticing the doctor's interest in the patient, paid her special attention. Mercedes did not know where she was and didn't care. She cried, not wanting to open her eyes. Although she could hear a woman's voice she couldn't quite hear what was being asked. Feeling a soft cold hand on her forehead, she instinctively opened her eyes. She could see a man blurred by her tears. After blinking, she made out a bald head and smiling eyes. He asked her something, but again the words were garbled. Mercedes wanted to ask about José but didn't dare because she didn't know who this man was. She closed her eyes again and kept them closed. She could remember everything. They had left her alone. She wanted to never have to open her eyes again. The sedatives had their desired effect. Later that evening Dr. Collado returned and confirmed, after consulting the X-rays, that the internal bleeding was under control. He came to speak to Mercedes.

"Don't be afraid, " he began. "You're safe here. This is a private clinic. We just need to ask you a few questions in order to fill out some official forms." Mercedes became frightened. She thought of the general and imagined that he'd be looking for her. Terrified, she looked at the doctor.

"Not the police."

Over the past week Dr. Collado had frequently heard that same plea from hospital patients. He knew very well what it meant. Mercedes' diminutive figure and her frightened eyes made him wonder what she could have done to deserve the savage beating that had been inflicted upon her. He tried to win her trust but Mercedes refused to talk. She only cried, especially when she learned that the doctor had found her next to a dead man. She knew it was José and from that moment on, she didn't want to live anymore. When the doctor told her she was lucky to be alive, she broke into tears.

CHAPTER 43

Finally, believing that she might actually be placing the doctor who had saved her life in danger, Mercedes told him about being tortured by General Gutiérrez' agents. She didn't reveal most of the events of her life though, because they embarrassed her.

Dr. Collado then understood the risk he was taking, but the threat of danger did not discourage him. On the contrary, Mercedes' appearance in his life had revived his sense of adventure which for years had been buried under the facade of the respectable gentleman he portrayed. He was glad Mercedes had not told anybody about what had happened to her. In the middle of one night he took her from the clinic and drove two hours to the summer home near the ocean that belonged to him and his wife. He left Mercedes there promising to stay in touch and making her promise not to speak to anybody. He reasoned that by not telling his wife anything, he was sheltering her from whatever trouble Mercedes was involved with. And there was more; Mercedes had awakened emotions in him that had long been dormant, given the monotony of his daily life. His wife noticed something different in the way he tossed in his dreams. She attributed it to the existing tension in the country, along with his insistence on having two jobs.

Mercedes accepted her new situation as if she had always lived in it. She wanted to contact José's family but followed the doctor's advice. He thought that it would be imprudent and that she might endanger everyone by doing so. She divided her time between lamenting her loneliness and embroidering, which she had learned in primary school. She embroidered anything to distract herself from her sadness. Life mattered very little to her, and she would have killed herself if she hadn't remembered the story she had heard as a child. She had been told the tale of a dead man who haunted the neighborhood by day and night because he had taken his own life. This was the only thing that kept her from hanging herself, because she could find no reason for living. Accustomed to the fact that no man had ever given her anything for nothing, she made herself up every day in anticipation of Dr. Collado's return. But during the entire time he sheltered her in his house he never asked for anything. When Mercedes decided to go back to the city to visit her mother, the doctor thought she was being unwise.

"I can't depend on you my entire life," Mercedes told the doctor firmly. "I'm fine now."

The doctor tried to dissuade her, but Mercedes' mind was made up. She didn't want to spend her entire life running away and besides, she assured the doctor, the general and his men thought she was dead.

"Leave me here. I live in the first courtyard," Mercedes directed him, thinking she might get him in trouble if he left her at her mother's front door.

"It doesn't matter to me. I can leave you at your house."

"No…it would attract too much attention."

He looked at her. She was an intelligent woman he thought.

It made him sad that she no longer depended on his care.

"I'll never forget what you did for me," Mercedes said to him, not knowing whether to hug him or to shake his hand. He looked at her and gave her a brotherly hug.

"I shall return to see you. Call me whenever you need me," he said as he watched her go. She looked young for her age. He breathed in deeply and left. Saddened, he couldn't rest that night.

CHAPTER 44

"I am a peasant woman," Lorenza told Doña Herminia when her daughter insisted on improving the way she dressed and her manner of speech. Doña Herminia was exasperated by her mother's stubbornness. Every time a friend came over to visit her, Lorenza would disappear. "I'm here for you. I don't need to see anyone else." Doña Herminia insisted that she meet her friends but actually felt relieved at not having the burden of introducing her as her mother. The day that she introduced Lorenza to her sisters she noticed how her mother's coarse appearance stood out in comparison to her sisters' elegant apparel. Little by little, however, something started to bother Doña Herminia that she couldn't pinpoint at first. She realized that she was beginning to be embarrassed, not by her mother's appearance, but by her own cowardice. She questioned her own lack of self-confidence and was irritated by the passivity with which she had carried on her entire life. She decided to test herself. Her first test case were her sisters. Hermi's sisters did not feel comfortable with Lorenza, but they didn't show it. They always greeted her amiably or inquired about her. One evening, Lorena found herself face to face with Lorenza, who was playing with Sara. After greeting her, she repeated what she had said the last time she had seen her:

"Tell me more about life in the countryside and the animals there."

Hermi, who was arriving at that moment, scolded her.

"Lorena, she has other things to talk about besides life in the country."

"Of course she does." Lorena replied, resenting Hermi's tone.

Lorenza, noticing the tension between the two sisters, excused herself and left the room. For Hermi it was her first triumph.

CHAPTER 45

When she opened the door, the first thing Luisa Valverde saw was the scar on her daughter's forehead. She let out a hoarse yell.

"I knew I would see you again," she said to Mercedes wiping her tears with her forearm. "José's brothers have been here almost every day. They've been looking for him everywhere… We figured that both of you had been killed. They even took the risk of going to your house and found it empty. If only you had listened to me…" Her mother's tone changed to the more accusatory one Mercedes was used to hearing.

Mercedes didn't say a word.

"It's good that you're alive," Luisa Valverde said, not knowing exactly how to handle her emotions. She was trying to be her usual blunt self.

"Where have you been all this time while the rest of us have been going crazy? How could you be so inconsiderate? And José…what happened to him?"

"They killed José," Mercedes answered impassively.

"Poor José!" Luisa lamented. "Poor child!"

Luisa saw Mercedes lie down on the bed and turn her back to her.

"Tomorrow we'll go to the country. We're not safe here," Mercedes could hear her mother saying. Luisa continued making plans aloud, but Mercedes was barely listening.

CHAPTER 46

The general returned to the house as if he had never left. He met his daughter who was now three months old. At first he looked at her coldly, but when he picked her up in his arms and saw her smile, he couldn't help but hug her. He sat in a rocking chair and looked at her closely. He then pronounced that she was his spitting image. He gave his wife a wet kiss and, smiling, asked her, "So when are you going to give me a son?"

Doña Herminia was used to the general's sudden mood swings, but the unexpectedness of his question left her speechless. Not knowing how to answer, she simply smiled. The general started to make plans for the little girl. The first thing was the name—he wanted to add the name Rosalía to her name in honor of his dead grandmother. Doña Herminia did not object because she knew it would be in vain. That night Doña Herminia cried quietly to herself. Sharing the bed with the general after almost a year of separation was terribly disconcerting. The general behaved more tenderly than she remembered. She responded to his caresses as she always had: automatically. When she felt the general inside her, she felt an uncontrollable urge to vomit. She couldn't sleep, thinking about how everything had so suddenly returned to normal. Making a mental effort, she placed recent events in chronological order. The situation in the country was under control her husband had said. She had thought that the general would reject her and her daughter, and she had been prepared to find another way of life. In the midst of her confusion, she had wanted the general to accept their daughter, but that had seemed like a remote possibility. Now the general was speaking as if he had always wanted to have children. She must, she told herself, accept that this is how things had changed. Her tears streamed while the deafening snores of the general tore through the silence.

The next day the general woke up in a good mood and promised her he'd be at home more often. He criticized the decor in his daughter's room and decided he had to buy her all new furniture.

"My daughter is not going to live like an orphan," he told her.

A few days later he himself took care of ordering new furnishings.

CHAPTER 47

Two days after the general's return Lorenza announced her plans to leave. Doña Herminia begged her to stay.

"The animals need my attention," Lorenza told her. "But if you need me I'm always there for you." Hermi hugged her and Lorenza caressed her silky black hair. It was the first time her daughter had surrendered to her. It seemed to her at that moment that Hermi was once again the baby she had taken to Pedro Casals with the idea of giving her a better future. Hermi timidly looked into Lorenza's eyes. Lorenza caressed her face.

"Everything is going to be all right, Hermi," she reassured her, sensing the confusion her daughter was feeling. "You'll see."

Hermi took a few steps backward, still not completely used to their new relationship.

"I wish I could go with you!" she exclaimed.

Lorenza, who had been trying to be strong, could no longer contain herself upon hearing those words. Her daughter was finally showing her that she loved her. She knew she could finally die in peace.

Her tears released the pain that had gnawed at her soul for all those years.

CHAPTER 48

Doña Herminia had started reading romance novels again, just as she had done before to dispel the boredom and solitude that preceded Sara's birth. She liked them because she'd lose track of time immersed in the plot. She anticipated the moment in which circumstances would bring the lovers together forever. Once she started reading a romance novel, she couldn't put it down, anxious to reach the end when the valiant hero, always capable of feeling both passion and tenderness, would overcome all obstacles keeping him from his beloved. The heroine was beautiful and shy, and she had loved the hero secretly since the day their eyes had met for the first time at the town carnival she was attending, protected by all the men in her family. Her chastity prevented her from confessing her true feelings because she was about to be married to the richest man in town, much older than she, but held in high regard by her entire family. He was, of course, the villain who obtained everything he wanted with his money and power and wasn't going to allow a young handsome stranger to take from him the most beautiful woman in town. Doña Herminia was in the middle of the first encounter of the two protagonists. The heroine risks everything to meet the man of her dreams in an old abandoned church. It is the first time they speak face to face because up to now all of their words had been exchanged by means of the burning intensity of their eyes. She surrenders to him without question. For a few moments Doña Herminia becomes the heroine. Absorbing the pleasure that the tale has left in her mind, she closes her eyes. When she opens them again she feels her own bed, which doesn't evoke special memories. The dreams she had when she got married had faded over time. For a long time she had waited for her husband all perfumed because she imagined that it was what all women did when they got married. But soon she realized that her husband couldn't care less how she awaited him.

She wanted to return to her reading but couldn't. Her eyes scanned the room she shared with the man they had married her to. She kept thinking without thinking of anything in particular. Without realizing it, she found herself thinking again about the events of her life.

She got out of bed and closed the book without marking the page as she usually did. Pacing the room, unable to stop her thoughts, she sat down only to get up again. Then she tasted blood in her mouth and touched her lips with her finger. It was bloodied because she had been biting the corner of her mouth unconsciously—a childhood habit that up to now she had managed to control. "How strange it is to feel trapped! To feel that the world is against you; that there is nowhere to go, and to feel so alone! What a horrible feeling! Terrible! To know that there's nothing left that can be done. Trying to make sense of all this so I don't lose my mind..."

CHAPTER 49

"Let me see, Grandma, let me see again," Sara was coaxing Lorenza to take out her dentures. Lorenza laughed and would remove them just to hear her granddaughter's enchanting laugh. Sara laughed and laughed. Lorenza, watching her, thought that Taní and the Baron of the cemetery had definitely been mistaken. Just in case though, she would light a candle at her altar every day to the spirits and to the saints, praying for her daughter's and granddaughter's happiness.

"Again, again," Sara begged.

"Sara, leave your grandmother alone," Doña Herminia said, watching them from the porch of Lorenza's house in the countryside.

"Oh, it doesn't bother me," Lorenza, who was now playing hide-and-seek with Sara, said.

Doña Herminia continued to observe her daughter. The short visits to her mother's house were the only times she felt her daughter was hers. Abelardo had taken over Sara, and she felt trapped. At first she had been happy to see the attention that the general had so unexpectedly lavished on the daughter she thought he would never accept. But the general did not give her a chance to be a mother; instead he would mock her in front of Sara, and Sara learned to turn to her father for everything. That is when Doña Herminia's hatred for the general began to grow.

"Mother, don't let Sara have the upper hand," she warned. She worried that her mother was too old to be running around so much.

They didn't listen to her. Upset, Doña Herminia got up and went into the house trying to find something that would distract her.

CHAPTER 50

"Here comes your old man," Luisa Valverde said to Mercedes.

Mercedes looked in the direction her mother was pointing and saw him walking toward the house with a spring in his step. His mustache was long and nicely groomed. He had flowers for Mercedes which she took after they hugged like old friends.

They both looked at Luisa Valverde leaving the house. Dr. Collado had been getting used to Luisa Valverde's changing moods. Some days she would greet him amiably; other days she'd ignore him. It no longer bothered him.

"Sit down doctor," said Mercedes, who had never stopped addressing him respectfully.

They sat down in silence. Mercedes was certain that Dr. Collado would expect something in return for all he had done for her. But he continued helping without asking for anything. First by hiding her and later by helping her set up the children's clothing store that gave her back control over her life. His visits were always brief as if to assure her that his intentions were honorable. Mercedes offered him lemonade and a towel to wipe the sweat from his brow. It wasn't hot but being so close to Mercedes made him nervous and this caused him to perspire profusely. He left after having the same conversation they always had, about how Mercedes' children's clothing store was doing, and the situation in the country.

Luisa Valverde returned to the house as soon as she saw him leave. She made herself a cup of coffee.

Mercedes picked up her knitting needles and began to knit. They sat in silence. After finishing her coffee, Luisa Valverde turned the empty cup upside down. Then she turned it up again and looked at what the random patterns foretold about her future. As usual they revealed very little.

As if speaking to herself, she said, "Men, they all want the same thing."

Mercedes continued to knit as if she hadn't heard.

"It's a shame to see him coming over here like an obedient dog. He will never dare to ask you for anything."

"And what do you want me to do about it?" Mercedes replied, accelerating her knitting.

"Why do you ask me when you don't pay attention to what I tell you?"

"Mother, for God's sake, let's not start!"

"You're using him. You should be ashamed."

Mercedes stood up and walked to another room for yarn she didn't need. She wanted to air out the fury her mother's words had stirred up in her.

"You can't stand the fact that someone loves me. Isn't that it, Mother?"

"I don't like seeing anyone being used. And you, with your little righteous face, are taking advantage of that man. Poor fellow, all these years giving with nothing in return."

"I've never asked him to do anything for me."

"Don't be a fool."

Mercedes began to sob.

"You want to drive me crazy. Leave me alone."

"The day I die."

Mercedes disappeared into the bedroom and threw herself on the bed.

"Stop acting like a spoiled child!" she heard her mother yell.

After a while Luisa Valverde walked into Mercedes' room and asked in a gentle voice, "Can I bring you coffee?"

Mercedes did not answer. Luisa brought the coffee over to her bedside.

"I don't want to make you cry," she said. "But who else can tell you these things? Don't be angry with me Mercedes, dear," Luisa Valverde murmured, tenderly stroking Mercedes' hair. Mercedes turned her head to face her mother, resigned to her sudden mood swings.

CHAPTER 51

When Doña Herminia received the news of her father's sudden death, she felt nothing. The tears refused to come. Standing before her father's coffin, she was revisited by the memories she had suppressed all those years. She relived every moment.

She remembered the hugs she needed from her father and never got and the words of praise she never heard. She went over and over each of the many times he had left her on her own, including her marriage and her stepmother. He never admitted anything, nor did he apologize for having handed her over to the general. On the contrary he behaved as if she had more luck than her sisters. Each memory was an example of how little her father had loved her. She would never forgive him. After the burial she finally was able to cry, and she cried all night wondering if her father had ever loved her.

CHAPTER 52

Sara enjoyed the frequent visits to her grandmother's house. There her mother seemed calmer and allowed her to go the beach like other kids her age.

It was during this time, when she was eight years old, that she started her friendship with Clarisa Medrano, the grocer's daughter. Her grandmother and mother allowed her to spend the night at Clarisa's house occasionally, and it was on one of these nights, the first summer they met, that they started a new game.

Sara and Clarisa played this game surreptitiously, behind closed doors. This lasted throughout the following two summers until one morning shame came knocking at their door. Cleaning themselves up as always, they got under the sheets and silently played with each other. Upon waking up they looked at each other and felt the guilt that produces conscious realization of the forbidden. That morning Clarisa threw off the sheets and sourly said, "We should be ashamed of ourselves."

Several nights later when Sara tried to cuddle against Clarisa's body as she had before Clarisa rejected her brusquely. Doña Herminia noticed the distance between the two friends that summer. When she asked Sara about it, all she could get was an indifferent "nothing" in response to her questions. Sara and Clarisa continued to see each other the following summers but they became aware of social differences that before had not concerned them. Childhood games were forgotten, and as time went by they became complete strangers.

CHAPTER 53

"Let's make me a son," the inebriated general announced one night.

"I'd rather slit my wrists than bring any son of yours into this world." Doña Herminia stood up to him firmly. He glared at her, hate in his eyes. Nothing infuriated him more than being rejected. He picked up the clothes he had taken off and went to sleep in another bedroom. From then on they stopped speaking to each other.

The happiness Doña Herminia had hoped to find in motherhood had gradually vanished. In Sara's mind her father was in charge and her mother had no authority. Doña Herminia accused the general of manipulating their daughter's love in his favor. She confronted him about all his infidelities and abusive behavior throughout their almost twenty years of marriage. The general tried to control her with the indifference that had paid off in the past, but it was in vain. Doña Herminia continued to defy him and the more frustrated she felt, the more openly she would reproach him. The reproaches turned into insults. The general accused her of being crazy. Desperate, Doña Herminia also faulted her daughter. She hounded her, accusing her of only loving her father. Sara, following her father's advice, ignored her mother.

Using the excuse of protecting Sara from his wife's constant nagging, the general took her everywhere, which only made Doña Herminia feel more alienated and lonely.

CHAPTER 54

What a false sense of security I'm feeling! This body that I inhabit moves and walks, but inside there is another; one that wants to scream, that does not want to live...hounded by my own despair. All these questions. All these things I don't have answers to. None of this makes any sense. I must do something. What is wrong with me today? I'm overwhelmed by so many doubts and so many questions.

Doña Herminia tried to make herself stop thinking, but she was powerless to do so. Her thoughts kept coming, each one waiting its turn. She turned again toward the mirror. On the surface her makeup hid the sleepless nights, but her will to live was gradually dying out. Taking a deep breath, she went out to celebrate her daughter's tenth birthday. In the photograph taken that day, the three of them appeared to be a happy family. Lorenza, who had come for the party, watched her daughter. She knew that Hermi didn't feel as radiant as she was pretending to be. It saddened her heart. Her little Sara had changed also; she no longer was interested in visiting her. Lorenza thought of Pedro Casals and blamed him for having forced her daughter into such a hell. "May God forgive him for all the evil he has done to so many people! And may God forgive me, but I'd give what is left of my life to see *this* man dead," she thought, watching the general playing with Sara.

CHAPTER 55

Doña Herminia had distanced herself from her family since Sara's birth. This included her cousin Raquel, who had always been her friend and was the closest to her among the family members. Cousin Raquel secretly harbored jealousy toward Lorenza because she felt Lorenza had stolen the place she had once held in Hermi's heart. They seldom saw each other, and when they did, they pretended that nothing had changed; but both knew that everything was different. Cousin Raquel was the one who most missed the years when they used to see or at least speak to each other almost daily. Raquel had been waiting patiently for Hermi to need her again, but Hermi simply did not show any interest in asking for help like before. Raquel was insulted by Hermi's indifference, especially when she remembered how much she had done for Hermi in the past. One afternoon, after almost five months had gone by without hearing from Hermi, Raquel decided to pay her an unannounced visit. She found Hermi lost in her thoughts, looking out her window at the doves flying into their dovecote. Doña Herminia received her coldly, without hiding the annoyance this unexpected visit had caused.

"Hermi, you have got to get out of this rut," Raquel cried out, in her characteristic dramatic tone.

Doña Herminia, to avoid having to explain herself, simply told her cousin that she hadn't been feeling too well lately. But her cousin knew her well enough to suspect another reason for her behavior.

"I can help you."

Hermi smiled ironically, which took Cousin Raquel by surprise.

"How does one make up for lost time, Raquel? How can

the lost years of my youth be recovered? No one can help me, but I am grateful that you have come to visit me."

"Aren't you worried about Sara?"

Tears flowed.

"Sara doesn't need me. She has her father."

Cousin Raquel didn't know what to do or what to say.

"You have to go out...do something."

Doña Herminia shrugged. "I don't care about anything anymore."

CHAPTER 56

It was early Sunday morning, and the general was waiting for his daughter to have breakfast. He saw her approaching and thought about how quickly she was growing up. She greeted him with a kiss. He held her by the waist and, looking into her eyes, said, "Tell me you love me."

"I love you lots, a whole lot," Sara told him while she hugged him again. He kissed her one more time. They had barely sat down when they saw Doña Herminia going toward the kitchen. She didn't speak to them.

"Go say hello to your mother," the general said. Sara looked at him, puzzled.

"Yes, go greet your mother," he repeated.

Sara went up to her mother and bade her good morning. Doña Herminia hugged her. For the first time ever Sara felt sorry for her. She looked toward her father reading the newspaper.

"Why don't you talk to him?" she asked her mother.

Doña Herminia shrugged.

"When you are older I'll explain it to you…have you had breakfast?" she asked her.

"Not yet…"

Sara looked at Doña Herminia, who was on the verge of tears. She was about to ask her to come with them to the beach that day; but then she thought that her father might think it wasn't such a good idea. She returned to her father's side. From there she saw her mother go by again, dragging behind her a robe that was too big for her. Sara looked at her father again and then looked back at where her mother had been.

CHAPTER 57

It was on one of those days when he accused her of being crazy that Doña Herminia with a smile the general did not recognize, said, "That is precisely what I want, to go crazy so I can kill you."

The coldness of her stare did not leave the general with any doubts of her intentions. He was convinced that Doña Herminia was becoming dangerous. He decided that he didn't feel safe leaving Sara in the house under her mother's care. That day, he decided to move out with his daughter to another one of his residences. They would do it gradually though, he explained to Sara, that way her mother wouldn't find out about it right away.

Doña Herminia did not make any effort to dispel the notion that she was going insane. She filled her room with materials for making rag dolls and stick dolls which she had learned to make at the boarding school. First she made a nativity scene, which won praise from those who saw it for the mastery with which she had woven the wires and sticks together. But she shocked everyone by surrounding baby Jesus with lots of little horned devils. Then she became fascinated with the devil's image and created many versions of him, which she hung all over her bedroom. The servants concluded that rather than being crazy, she was possessed. The day the general removed the last of his belongings from the house, he said to Hermi, "I'm moving out so I won't be forced to place you in an insane asylum." Doña Herminia didn't care. At first Sara stayed over a few nights because she felt badly about leaving her mother. Afterwards she stayed less and less until she was only coming over once a week. Doña Herminia spent hour after hour touching every wall of the house pursuing dust and hidden filth. Finally the two maids who had served her for years could no longer bear their mistress' transformation. She had become unreasonable and demanding, and when they announced they were leaving, Doña Herminia said simply, "I understand." Then she removed all of her belongings from the closet and offered them to the women. They refused to take her clothes, feeling they would be taking advantage of an insane woman. But Doña Herminia, guessing what was restraining them, said, "But, how silly can you be? Don't you realize how wealthy I am?" Moved, the maids changed their minds and said they wanted to stay. But Doña Herminia yelled that she didn't want to ever see them or anyone anymore. She locked herself up in the house.

CHAPTER 58

Sara wrote to her grandmother shortly after the maids left the house. As soon as Lorenza received the letter she prepared to leave. She left her neighbor Hemilda in charge of her house and her animals. "I have a feeling I won't be back for a while," she told her. "Make yourself at home."

Hemilda reminded Lorenza to take care of herself because, for years, she had been bothered with stomach problems which she had kept from her daughter. Lorenza arrived at Doña Herminia's doorstep about five days after the maids had left. She was surprised to see the entrance unlocked and unguarded. She rang the bell several times but no one answered. She feared the worst. Then an old cadaverous man approached her. He introduced himself as the new watchman assigned to the main entrance. Lorenza asked about Doña Herminia, and he just shrugged.

"I've been here several months, but I've never seen her leave," he said. "I know she's there because the lights stay on till very late at night."

Lorenza began to call her name. It took a while for Hermi to open the door. The watchman excused himself, "I'm the new watchman and I'm here to serve you."

Wearily Hermi looked at her mother and did not give her the customary hug.

"Angel, what has happened to you!"

Hermi looked right through her.

"Nothing... I'm doing what I please and because of that they say I'm crazy." She laughed. "I feel more normal than ever. What are you doing here?"

"I'm here to be with you."

They walked through the hallway that led to the main living room. All the drapes and blinds were drawn shut. It was stifling hot because the air conditioner had been turned off.

"This darkness, Herminia, is bound to affect you," Lorenza said.

"Nothing bothers me at all. Not my daughter, not my husband, nobody."

Lorenza looked her over. She knew Hermi had been going through tough times, but she was not prepared for her daughter's lost stare and unkempt appearance. Lorenza switched her tone of voice from amazement to a normal pitch.

"Now tell me what has happened with Sara and Abelardo?"

"Well what do you think? It bothered him that I have been painting the devil."

Lorenza suppressed her shock. They stopped in the middle of the living room.

"Look" she said, pointing to the walls.

Hung like Christmas decorations were all sorts of devils made of little sticks and wires wearing sombreros and on horseback.

Lorenza laughed. Hermi joined in, giggling uncontrollably.

"Those are the loveliest devils I've ever seen in my life."

Hermi stopped laughing. "Do you think I'm crazy?"

Lorenza looked at her with moist eyes. She took Hermi's hands and caressed them.

"No, sweetheart...only very sad."

They embraced.

CHAPTER 59

Eulogio Valdez was accustomed to seeing personalities change before the camera lens. It wasn't something he could prove scientifically, but he saw it every time he photographed people. At times he'd capture the image while the subject was still undergoing the unconscious transformation. It never failed. His client would then reject the photograph saying, "That doesn't look like me." He had concluded that, in spite of the existence of mirrors, people never saw themselves as they really were. A person's self-image was nothing more than a mentally constructed projection and that is why the signs of age went unnoticed. He saw the general's daughter enter, appearing shy and disoriented. She was tall and slender and had the face of a frightened little puppy. Aiming the camera, he took a picture. The flash blinded her momentarily. Afterwards he watched her walk across the room, straightening her shoulders and tightening her body. When she took her father's hand, Eulogio Valdez witnessed a transformation. If at first she had looked younger than her sixteen years, now she looked older.

He followed her the rest of the night and watched her phase in and out of that transmutation.

Sara was giving him instructions on how she wanted the photographs to be taken. Her tone was authoritarian and self-assured. To her he was simply a photographer, a man with a camera who was to serve her the way everybody else did. Sara noticed the photographer's inquisitive look. Something in his eyes made her feel insecure. She was not used to a man's gaze. Seeing him for the first time for what he really was—a young, good-looking man, she began asking him for his opinion instead of giving him orders. As he took more photos he explained the best compositions and told her he worked as a reporter who only photographed social events on occasion.

From a distance the general watched Sara chatting with the photographer. He always felt uneasy whenever he saw his daughter near any man, no matter who he was. His palms sweating, he signaled to one of his bodyguards to approach.

"Who recommended the photographer?" he asked.

"Benito, sir. Would you like me to ask him to come?"

"No, no...never mind. If he contracted him, he must be trustworthy."

He was bothered by the man's youth and that his Sara smiled at him so much. He waited, watching her pose coquettishly for the next photograph. Not able to stand it any longer, he walked up to them. Ignoring the photographer and taking his daughter by the arm, speaking only to her, he said, "Well my princess you have spent the entire evening being photographed."

The general realized that he wasn't welcome. He shot the photographer a quick glance as though he were afraid of finding something he didn't want to see.

"Just one more," Sara said. "Take one here now, with my father."

The photographer snapped another photograph with a smile but without much enthusiasm.

Sara left on her father's arm, without saying good-bye.

A man dressed in black approached the photographer.

"You may leave. Señorita Gutiérrez has had enough photographs taken for tonight. Benito will get back to you about picking them up."

The photographer left, thinking, "They have a way of making a person feel like dirt."

CHAPTER 60

One night Doña Herminia had a dream. She dreamt of two caged dogs. Through the wires of the cage she could see their teeth gleaming. They were barking. She approached them fearfully. Their fetid breath enveloped her. Nauseated, she ran, trying to escape. She couldn't. Helpless, she crouched: head between her legs, hands pressed against her head, locked in a fetal position. She stayed this way until she opened her eyes. Then she saw an endless line of old men wrapped in a cloud of dust, walking toward her slowly, covered from head to toe in a yellow hooded garb stained with saltpeter. They approached slowly, revealing long toes made scaly by the sun. They had to be friars of some order because their vestments reminded her of a saint she had seen but whose name she couldn't remember. She heard them play instruments she couldn't identify. Then she saw little tin cans in their hands and realized that the sound was coming from the jingling coins inside them and not from a musical instrument as she had initially thought. The old men were whispering something and pointing at her. Then they ran toward her. They were going to smother her. She could read it in the shining points of light that were their eyes. Now she realized they weren't friars but street people.

Once on top of her, she saw they were no longer just old men but also old women, children, and women with newborns in their arms. Their faces were grotesquely enlarged as if she were seeing them through a magnifying glass.

The coins kept hitting the sides of the tins with frantic persistence. She covered her face squeezing her eyes shut until they hurt. But that didn't keep her from seeing their rotten gums and decayed teeth gnawing on her flesh. Agitated she woke up. She sniffed her body searching for the source of the smell she could still detect. Perspiring, despite the air conditioning in her room, she reviewed the images from the dream over and over again. When she got up she told her mother about it.

"This is a dream that lends itself to many interpretations," Lorenza told her and didn't want to say more because the dream bore all the symbols of destruction. Lorenza prayed that night to the spirits she knew and to all the saints, that if someone had to die, that it be she, not her daughter or granddaughter.

CHAPTER 61

Cousin Raquel became Sara's mentor and played the role of mother every time she had the opportunity. The general appreciated it because many times he was gone and he counted on Raquel to watch and care for "his treasure," as he referred to Sara. Everyone treated Sara like a victim because of her mother's condition. Cousin Raquel, who remained Hermi's staunch defender, exclaimed upon hearing that Doña Herminia had dyed her hair red: "She really isn't crazy. She has just become eccentric." No one, Sara thought, wanted to face the fact that someone in the family was insane.

One afternoon, while visiting her mother, Sara noticed that Doña Herminia was talking more than usual. She was asking Sara about what she was doing and about the school for young ladies she was attending. Sara answered in monosyllables while looking at her mother's red hair. "She looks horrible," Sara thought. She then asked her grandmother why she had allowed her mother to dye her hair.

"She has the right to do whatever she wants," Lorenza said.

Sara turned to her and in a stern, authoritative tone said, "And you give her too much encouragement."

"Why don't you visit us more often?" Lorenza asked, ignoring her granddaughter's hardened tone. "It really hurts your mother that you don't come by, though she would never admit it."

"I have a lot to do in school," Sara answered.

Sara knew her grandmother disapproved of her behavior, but she didn't know what else to do. It was impossible to talk about anything interesting with her mother. She was always asking the same questions. When Sara left, Lorenza noticed that Hermi looked very sad.

"Why did you abandon me, Mom?" she asked.

Lorenza was taken by surprise.

"I did not abandon you," she replied. "I thought you'd be better off with your father. Now I don't know...but it's too late to cry over it."

Hermi watched the doves fly back and forth from the dovecote.

CHAPTER 62

Sara had been thinking about how to ask her father for permission to go to her friend Josefina's birthday party. Josefina, the daughter of a diplomat, was a friend from school. Sara was attracted to Josefina's assertive personality and the freedom she had. As soon as her father came home, she asked him for permission to attend the party. Distracted by other matters, the general offhandedly said that he would have to think it over because he didn't have an available escort to take her.

Desperate, Sara said, "You can take me." knowing that the general was just making up excuses to keep her from going.

"When are you going to realize that you aren't just anybody's daughter? That you just can't go flitting about like a bird from party to party."

"But I never go anywhere. You won't ever let me do anything."

His lips trembling, he said, "Stop talking back."

Sara gave him a resentful look, then locked herself in her bedroom to cry. She missed the freedom she had when she lived in the country with her grandmother and mother. Her father never even let her spend the night with her friends. The general did not like his daughter's new friend from the moment he met her. He had been observing her, and despite the fact that she came from a good family, she exerted a negative influence on Sara. Prior to associating with Josefina, Sara had never gone against her father's wishes. Now things were different. He decided he was going to forbid his daughter from seeing Josefina again.

That night, still hoping that her father would let her go out, she joined him at dinner time. Her eyes were swollen from crying, and she wanted to make sure that the general noticed her unhappiness. They dined in silence. Sara would look at her father out of the corner of her eyes, but the general appeared distracted. He had never for a moment considered letting her go to the party. Instead, he was planning to find a way to keep her away from her new friend.

When Sara stood up from the table, he told her, "It isn't a safe place. We can't go."

Sara let out a dejected wail. She ran to her room. The general ran behind her, grabbed her arm and forced her to look at him.

"I'm doing this to protect you. It's for your own good."

Frightened, Sara sobbed. Her father's face was transformed by rage. The general saw panic in his daughter's eyes. That hurt him. He let her go. Sara slammed the door to her room. Suddenly pensive, the general tried to compare his daughter's behavior with that of earlier days. Fragments of past conversations with his daughter revisited him.

"Promise me that you'll never leave me."

"Never, Daddy. Never."

CHAPTER 63

The general and those who supported him had managed to stay in power for almost thirty years, running the country under the guise of democracy. Democratic elections had taken place over the past fifteen years since the last public demonstrations and consequent repression. In the final account, however, the military ensured that the right person was elected. The people would then protest for a few days, raising accusations of bought votes and fraud. Then, disillusioned, they would return to their houses and prepare themselves for the next four years. The majority opted for the peace that the military offered in exchange for good conduct. Under this mutual agreement the country enjoyed economic progress. The generation raised during this purchased peace did not remember the mass repressions or the disappearances with which the military government effectively silenced the people. They wanted more freedom of speech, more explanations for why things were as they were and more changes. The military watched this new generation of "rebels," as General Gutiérrez called them, very closely. But it wasn't just the new generation that dreamed of change; some of the rank and file also wanted to establish a new order. It was this atmosphere that bred an idea that previously would have been rejected as impossible: the assassination of General Abelardo Gutiérrez. The plan was masterminded by one of the general's closest collaborators.

General Gutiérrez had demanded and received absolute obedience from his immediate collaborators for many years. He controlled many of them by putting into practice the principle that it was better to kill an innocent person than to allow a traitor to escape. Others were compromised in such a way that their lives and those of their families literally depended on him. In times of doubt he would remind himself, "If I disappear, so will they." The fact that the situation was changing and the perception that the general had lost much of his former control propelled the moment that many had died waiting for. The ringleaders of the plan represented two different generations: General Alberto Ruiz, from the general's immediate circle, who for years had remained overshadowed by General Gutiérrez, and lieutenant colonel Juan Marina Duarte, who had hated the general since his best friend and military school companion had been accused of treason and then executed. Alberto Ruiz also wanted to make the general pay for countless degrading humiliations. At first the plan was to assassinate the general, but over time the idea underwent modifications. With Ruiz in power, General Gutiérrez could be publicly accused for all the atrocities that had been carried out, and, if they were lucky, condemned to death by popular acclaim. Ruiz would present himself as the leader of a faction of the military committed to purging the army of corruption and returning control to the people. It was decided that the general would be more useful kidnapped and alive. Besides, he could always be killed later. As a crucial part of the plot they were counting on the participation of the general's personal dentist, Dr. Mariano Pérez. It was he who would confirm, based on the dental remains, that the general had died when his airplane crashed and burned while supposedly traveling to the country's inland provinces. Since it was a trip that the general frequently made, no one would question it.

For Dr. Mariano, participating in the conspiracy against the general wasn't a question of political ambition, but instead a way to redeem and liberate himself from the guilt the general had burdened him with when he was forced to extract prisoner's teeth without anesthesia. He would never forget the prisoners' wretched screams. Often he both admired and despised the men he tortured because, even if he had wanted to, he lacked the courage to rebel as they had. The opportunity to take charge and to avenge himself at the same time had finally arrived.

CHAPTER 64

"I have nothing to say to them," Hermi told Lorenza when she announced that her two sisters were waiting for her in the living room.

"They have come many times to visit you."

"I don't want to see anybody. Don't insist Mother," Doña Herminia pleaded as she braided a rag doll's hair.

Lorenza was saddened by all this because, except for her, no one doubted that her daughter was crazy. "May it be God's will," she thought as she bade the two sisters good-bye while they shot glances at Hermi's bedroom door.

"Tell her that we love her very much and think about her all the time," said Laura, who lately had been feeling guilty over her past treatment of Hermi. On their way to their respective homes they commented that someone should do something because the situation had gone on long enough. The only one who could make a decision was the general and he didn't appear to be interested. Even Lorenza was losing hope that her daughter was ever going to come back from the world to which she had retreated. She had been waiting for a miracle but Doña Herminia seemed to be less willing to speak to her every day. In any event Lorenza was prepared to care for her until the end. She had waited a long time for this privilege. She was wrapped up in these thoughts when she heard the doorbell ring. She figured that Hermi's sisters had forgotten something. But it was the night watchman.

"May God keep him in His glory, Doña Lorenza!" the night watchman said as he removed his hat in a gesture of respect. "The ways of the world! One day you're alive, and when you least expect it life is over. Just like that."

"Don Ramiro what's going on ?" Lorenza asked, alarmed.

Ramiro looked at her embarrassed. His sorrowful tone

changed to one of urgency.

"Haven't you heard? It's all over the radio...the general is dead. He fell in one of those planes..." He told her, pointing to the sky.

"Are you sure?"

Lorenza's first impulse was to run to Hermi. She entered her daughter's room. Hermi, her back facing the door, was stooped over, working on her dolls as if her life depended on it. She tried to imagine Hermi's reaction. "Could it be true?" she hesitated. She walked around to face her daughter.

"Hermi," she called out. But Doña Herminia continued to painstakingly place a little hand on one of her dolls. "Hermi darling, they say that the general is dead. An airplane accident. Ramiro has just told me."

Doña Herminia paused momentarily without raising her eyes.

"It has to be a hoax...one of his political maneuvers," she said, her eyes still focused on her work.

"But if it's true, we should be with Sara," Lorenza said.

"Call Raquel...she'll know."

"But sweetheart, you've had all of the phones disconnected. We have no radio, no telephone, nothing. My God, we don't find out about anything," Lorenza lamented, feeling all the more desperate given the calmness with which her daughter had taken the news.

"It's not possible," Hermi said.

"Look, let's ask Ramiro to bring us a radio."

"He controls the radio too...he controls everything."

"I want to go to Sara. She needs us."

"No," Hermi said, still concentrating on the little hands she was attaching to one of the stick dolls. "She will come when she needs us."

Lorenza started to cry.

"Please don't make the same mistake I made, for God's sake."

"We will talk later," Hermi answered as if she hadn't heard her.

After her mother left the bedroom, Hermi stood in front of the mirror. It had been a long time since she had looked at herself. Older and paler she barely recognized herself. She lay down and tried not to allow herself to think, as she had done for so many years. But it was no longer possible. What her mother had said still echoed in the room. From deep within herself came the resonance of her own voice. "To begin again, where and for what purpose?"

CHAPTER 65

"If hell exists, that one's going straight to it," Luisa Valverde said, glued to the radio, listening to the latest bulletins on the general's death. "You should go out to celebrate."

"I'm not one to party," Mercedes said.

"Now who can understand you? You've been scared to even go to the bathroom, and now that this devil is dead, you pretend it's not important. I don't understand you."

Mercedes didn't answer because, once her mother got started, it didn't matter what she said. Luisa Valverde continued talking, oblivious to whether Mercedes was listening or not.

"No one can convince me that God exists. Where is the justice in him dying so suddenly? I would have wanted him to suffer more to pay for all the evil he has done. But who knows? Maybe he was alive after the fire. Now that would be something."

She broke into a cackle that revealed her teeth blackened from the pipe she smoked.

"For God's sake, Mama, don't speak of the dead like that!"

"I'm not afraid of anything," Luisa said. "Not of heaven nor hell. Hell is here for me and let God keep heaven because I'm not interested in it."

"Be quiet. People might hear you."

Luisa Valverde spoke louder.

"Everybody knows I'm an atheist. I don't deny it! At least I'm not a hypocrite like all of those out there…they go to church but then you watch how they treat others."

She continued to talk as if speaking to herself.

"If God existed he would not have allowed you to suffer so much. What did we ever do to deserve to be treated so unfairly? No, to me he is an unjust God."

CHAPTER 66

General Alberto Ruiz had one shining moment before the television cameras, lamenting the general's death and promising to maintain public order. The many cells within the army that General Gutiérrez kept in check erupted everywhere. Various warring factions emerged. General Alberto Ruiz was found dead, shot through the forehead. The puppet government, supported by General Gutiérrez, resigned in the midst of massive demonstrations staged everywhere. A provisional government comprised of one military man and two civilians was formed. To pacify the populace, the triumvirate promised to bring to justice those who were guilty of the imprisonments and disappearances during the reign of the military regime and the figurehead presidents.

Since Alberto Ruiz's assassination, Juan Marina Duarte, the other ringleader involved in kidnapping the general, remained hidden. As the situation worsened he did what many others did—fled the country with everything he could take. "It didn't happen the way it was supposed to," he thought, now that he felt safe. He had imagined another ending, a glorious ending. Everything had happened so quickly. They had calculated the kidnapping and alleged death of the general in minute detail but they had not anticipated the strength of the suppressed resentment among the people, nor the degree of ambition among the generals who had lived under General Gutiérrez's shadow. Alberto Ruiz's assassination, the work of fellow military men, was proof of that. Juan Marina Duarte took with him the secret of General Gutiérrez's whereabouts. He was satisfied that the major on duty would follow orders to kill the general should something go wrong. But the fact that he had not directly communicated with the major deeply concerned him.

CHAPTER 67

Dr. Mariano Pérez's misfortune was that it took him so long to make a decision that when he finally made one it was already too late. The first days after the general's death, he didn't have any contact with the ringleaders who had recruited him. That was the agreement they had made to prevent suspicion. At first Alberto Ruiz's assassination had kept him awake at night, but later he calmed down thinking that soon Juan Marina Duarte would contact him. But Juan Marina Duarte was far from thinking of the poor dentist whose account had convinced the entire world that the dental remains, which really belonged to two political prisoners, were those of the general and his personal pilot. Nervously he lit one cigarette after another, transforming his home into a suffocating smoked-filled prison. His wife, who did not have the least idea of how much he was suffering, attributed his behavior to his close relationship to the general and to the courtroom summons that the new government had started to make. She reassured him confidently more than once that he didn't have to worry because everyone knew that he had been the general's dentist and nothing more. His wife's attempts at calming him down only made him feel more isolated. She didn't have the slightest idea of the fear and nightmares that were consuming him. The day the newspapers reported that among those who were going to court was Aquilino Ramírez, the general's personal architect, Dr. Mariano knew he would be next. In a moment of desperation, he considered confessing the truth about his involvement in the general's death. It would make his story about being forced to torture people more believable. He decided to do it after he realized that Juan Marina Duarte had left him to fend for himself. He asked for an audience with the ruling body but such requests arrived daily, so he did not receive an answer. He decided to tell his story to the army's new commander who was reputed to be an honest man. The poor doctor's lot had been drawn. The commander could not receive him. Instead, one of his assistants did. Alfredo Coronado was an ex-navy captain who had served under General Gutiérrez and who was now collaborating with the new government. Dr. Mariano refused to talk to him. The captain tried amiably to convince him that he could confide in him, but Dr. Mariano was no longer confiding in anyone. He said good-bye. The captain accompanied him to the door and from there watched him disappear down the hallway.

CHAPTER 68

If previously the secret world surrounding the general was strange and unfamiliar to Doña Herminia, after his death it became even more incomprehensible. For her daughter's sake, she felt it was necessary to know more about her husband's accident, but she ran into a wall of impenetrable silence. The people who had been in her husband's immediate circle suddenly would not return her calls. She looked again at the picture of the woman in the cover story of the newspaper. The woman was pointing to a scar on her knee and providing details of how they had pierced her knee with a live wire. "The best thing to do would be to leave and go abroad, far away from all of this. But I don't know...each day that goes by is another nightmare that I cannot wake up from. If only I could forget everything. I have to find out who I am. Where have I been all these years?...I must take control of this fleeting time that moves forward despite my apprehensions. I must go on. Go on with my eyes closed. Go on and not ask why. Go on until I die...I feel so lost!"

She could not believe or accept that she herself had no idea about anything that had been going on. She scrutinized her memory for clues that would reveal something about the deaths and tortures that were now being attributed to the general.

CHAPTER 69

Eyes dilated with rage, Luisa Valverde jumped up. Paulina, her next door neighbor, had just informed her that one of their neighbors had been spreading nasty rumors about Mercedes.

"I'm telling it to you, my dear, the way I heard it. The very same way...Carmen is going around saying that your daughter was one of the general's women...In this town and at this time that can be dangerous," Paulina repeated, hoping to get even more of a reaction from Luisa.

"That whore now thinks she's the Virgin Mary," Luisa Valverde shouted so the entire neighborhood could hear her.

"Mama the best thing is not to pay attention," advised Mercedes, who had been listening to the conversation.

"That rat who was living off leftovers now thinks she's rich. Let her come and tell me to my face and then we'll decide who's who."

"Mama, that's enough, for God's sake."

"Your mother is right my dear. These rumors have to be nipped in the bud," the old woman Paulina said, excited over Luisa Valverde's outrage.

"I am not like you," Luisa retorted to her daughter. "I don't let everyone walk all over me. That Carmen better not let me see her face because I'll show her what it means to go around insulting my family."

Paula shifted restlessly. She was committing Luisa's exact words to memory so that as soon as she saw Carmen she could warn her about the impending danger she was in. Each time Luisa voiced another threat Paulina nodded her head in approval. The old woman didn't do anything else in her life but listen to and repeat neighborhood gossip. She was certain of the worthy service she provided for everybody.

CHAPTER 70

"I don't know who you are anymore Hermi," said Cousin Raquel.

Doña Herminia looked at her for a while before answering. She knew that Raquel wanted to help her, and she also knew that Raquel could not get used to the idea that she was perfectly capable of making her own decisions. "That's what is really bothering Raquel," she thought.

"I don't want to spend my life running away like I've been doing for so many years. We're going to stay here."

"Sara is deeply troubled by all these revelations about the general. You're not thinking of her."

"Sara is the only one I think about." Her eyes welled with tears.

Raquel looked at her, scrutinizing the eyes that had lost their familiar shyness. There was something in those eyes now that called for respect, or even fear. For a second she thought what she had not wanted to admit to herself: that maybe Hermi was indeed insane. Raquel continued to insist on the trip abroad.

"At least until things quiet down," she pleaded.

Doña Herminia smiled sardonically.

"Thank you. You know you are still my guardian angel, Raquel. But I have made up my mind. We will get away from all this, but not by leaving the country."

CHAPTER 71

A cross was slowly being traced into his forehead with a lighted cigarette. The wrinkles on the poor dentist's face swelled up. All of his veins cried out in silent pain.

He was being judged for treason. When two men forced him into a car in broad daylight, he momentarily hoped that maybe, finally, Juan Marina Duarte had decided to get in touch with him. However, he soon realized that the way his kidnappers were treating him was far from friendly. The captain he met during his brief visit to the courthouse had deduced that, since Dr. Mariano had been the general's personal dentist, he might be able to provide prejudicial information about some of his comrades. But the doctor, whose threshold for pain was very low, immediately confessed, never knowing exactly which faction of the army he was talking to. He said everything he knew, providing the few details he was certain of.

The assailants' reactions covered the spectrum: from amazement to vengeance to an ultimate feeling of worthlessness because the information that the doctor was giving them was too fragmented, too late. The remote possibility that the general could still be alive had them hoping for a while until they realized that without concrete information they would never be able to convince those who were still loyal to the general to take a risk given the current situation.

Doctor Mariano had no hope and did not delude himself into thinking he would come out of this predicament alive. He knew the cruelty of the men who supported the general. The only prayer he had was that they would not carry out their threat to torture his daughter and wife. "That would be the worst thing that could happen," he thought. "God did not have the right to make them pay for his sin," So he begged them more than once while the torturers amused themselves aiming at his forehead and cocking the trigger. The doctor twitched nervously with each click. After a while he heard them moving away. He instinctively peered through the only eye that would open. He saw the three aiming at him from a distance. It was the last thing he saw.

CHAPTER 72

"If you want it I'm happy for you to have it," said Lorena looking at her other sister from the corner of her eye.

"I'll pay you both for the farm, what is due to you, as soon as the government lifts the encumbrance on my houses."

"I think you should fight for the beach palace. It's such a beautiful piece of property. It would really be a shame for you to lose it."

Doña Herminia had listened to those same opinions from her family over and over. She chose not to answer this time. Then Laura intervened, "I don't see why you want to isolate yourself like this, on this farm. If anything were to happen to you, we'd never find out."

"Two hours isn't that much," she said, just to say something.

"I don't know...Given the political situation and your own condition..." Lorena's voice trailed in reaction to the look she received from Doña Herminia.

Doña Herminia rose saying that she had to go. She thanked them for the coffee while the two sisters protested, "What? So soon?"

"I want to get back to the farm before nightfall."

"You're going back today?"

"Hermi, for God's sake, stay in my house tonight. It's dangerous out there."

"Or in mine."

"I really appreciate your concern," Hermi said, tired of the formalities and pleasantries that she knew by heart. "The triumvirate seems to have everything under control...I really can't complain. They've treated me with a lot of respect."

She didn't let them continue and said good-bye.

After they closed the door Lorena said, "She really seems to be okay."

"Yes but who in their right mind would go and live on that weed-filled farm? Don't you remember the condition the house is in? It's falling apart."

"Well, as far as I'm concerned, I hope she doesn't change her mind and does buy us out from our share," Lorena calculated.

"Money is all you think about. Poor Hermi. I'm not at all convinced that she is not still crazy."

CHAPTER 73

"She thinks her Daddy is still in control," Alexandra smirked as Sara passed by. Alexandra had been a friend, in fact one of her best friends. But Sara had discarded her when she became friends with Josefina, the diplomat's daughter. Alexandra was getting back at her now. She had joined the group that had always resented the privileges enjoyed by the daughters of those who were in power.

In the private school where she studied, Sara had known only favoritism because she was General Gutiérrez's daughter. When classes started again, after her father's death, Sara entered a new world. It began with notes left on her desk, accusing her of being a murderer's daughter, followed by direct accusations, until even the teachers, who had indulged her before, now completely ignored her.

Her circle of friends was reduced, even among the daughters of the military men. Sara defended herself and her father, but the group of accusers grew daily. The idea her mother had of living on Aunt Florencia's farm, which initially had seemed ridiculous, was becoming increasingly more appealing. It was her only way to escape the torment she was undergoing at school.

CHAPTER 74

Reeking from not having bathed in days, and wearing ragged pants, General Gutiérrez was trying to get some sleep. His weakened condition kept him somewhere between a dormant and a semiconscious state. Images floated at a distance as if he were dreaming. At times he could envision the shooting and the place where he was ambushed, and then every blood vessel in his body would fill to bursting. Filled with rage by these memories, he would experience moments of complete lucidity. It was at those times that he realized he had to sleep in order to regain his strength. He tried counting sheep like his grandmother had taught him, and to get as comfortable as he could on the mat he had to sleep on. Before drifting off, he concluded that one could get accustomed to anything in life. After all who would have thought that he could sleep with his arms tied behind his back? He woke up the next morning feeling he had slept well for the first time since being taken captive. He didn't know where he was or how long he had been there, or what day of the week it was. By the overall silence and the chirping birds, he figured out he was far from the city. The moderate temperature, bordering on cold, led him to believe that he was in the mountains.

CHAPTER 75

Their commander had left them on an abandoned farm with strict orders to watch the prisoner and not to speak to him under any circumstances. He had assured them they would be relieved in a few days. But the days turned to weeks. The last time they saw him, he was accompanied by two men who moved like ghosts in the darkness. The men had not budged from their spot, but provisions were scarcer as the days went by. That's when El Gato and El Gordo, the nicknames these recruits were known by, decided it was time to get in touch with the commanding base in town where the commander who had given them the orders to watch the prisoner was stationed. El Gato made the trip in two days and found everything changed. The battalion to which he and El Gordo had belonged had moved to another position, and the commander that had left him and his friend in the mountain had been replaced by someone else. El Gato wasn't very bright, but he realized then that his commander had left them on their own. The only thing he could think of doing was to run back to the hideout in the mountains to alert his friend. He was so frightened that his own shadow made him jump.

"They screwed us, man," he said, his voice shaking.

"What bothers me the most is the promotion they promised us...we've been here all this time going hungry, killing mosquitoes, for nothing.

"That's how it goes, I guess. What should we do with the old man?"

"Let's go see him."

They studied him carefully as if this were the first time they had seen him. They removed the gag which they had stuffed in his mouth as a punishment because the general had spit at them.

They hadn't brought food and they weren't aiming their guns at him as they usually did. Realizing that something had changed, the general altered his approach. He tried to think of something to say that would anger and confuse them.

"Those commanders of yours who left you here...Looks like they forgot you."

The recruits didn't answer.

The general continued, "If you help me, you will be heroes. Besides, I promise to reward you well for your efforts."

They looked at each other, smiling nervously.

"We may be from the country, but we ain't stupid."

Then El Gato, signaling to El Gordo to follow him, went outside. The general strained to hear what they were saying, but the two recruits were whispering.

"Do you think it's true?" asked El Gato, flustered.

"How am I supposed to know?"

"Either way, we're screwed."

"And the old geezer can recognize us now."

They walked back in.

The general asked casually, "What are the newspapers saying about me?"

"We don't get newspapers here, and the closest town is two days away. But people are saying that you burned up in an airplane crash."

"So that's what they're saying," he muttered to himself. Becoming upset he continued, "What else do they say?"

The recruits looked at each other.

"Well, we don't know much. Yesterday when I went into town they told me that the capital is in an uproar, that Porfirio Asunción's government is in exile...and that there is a new government now..."

The general remained silent. The news shocked and depressed him.

"Damn those sons of bitches. Come on, tell me, damn it. Who brought you here?"

Jerking his arms trying to untie his hands, he was consumed with rage. The veins along his throat protruded viciously. They were swollen and full of blood. Suddenly unintelligible guttural squeals came out of his mouth. His face transfixed, the volcanic forces of his frustrations gathered strength in his chest, roaring and about to explode. Horrified, the recruits forgot that he was the prisoner and that they were in control. They fled while the general howled. Outside the recruits tried to decide what to do.

"We're about to get ourselves in big trouble...He may make us promises now, but if we let him go...What do you think?"

"The first thing that he'll do is have us shot. I don't want to risk it."

"Me neither."

They walked back in and couldn't believe what they were seeing.

CHAPTER 76

"How can you believe those lies?" Sara asked her mother. Doña Herminia had decided that it was time to broach the subject with Sara.

"I don't know whether to believe them or not. In any case, we have to talk."

"My father was an honorable man." Eyes on fire, Sara glared at her mother suspiciously. "If you're going to try to convince me that he did all that they are saying...forget it. Anyway, I know you never loved him, and," she added, "you didn't shed one tear when he died."

The look in her daughter's eyes terrified her. It was the same one she had so often seen in the general's eyes. She began to feel as she used to feel before the general: speechless and helpless. She made a conscious effort to ignore the coldness in Sara's tone of voice.

"Why are you treating me like this, Sara? What happened is not my fault."

Sara looked at her mother, choking back the tears.

"It may as well be. Not a Mass, nothing. You haven't attempted to defend him from all these lies," she threw herself on her bed, sobbing.

Doña Herminia approached the bed and sat down next to her. She caressed her hair.

"There's nothing we can do, Sara. The situation is dangerous, even for us..."

Sara moved her head away, rejecting her mother's touch.

CHAPTER 77

"I don't understand why you work so hard," Lorenza said to her, coming to announce that lunch was ready.

"These coffee trees are going to produce once more," she announced to her mother enthusiastically.

"You're wealthy enough to live off what you have. You surely do not need to exhaust yourself working," Lorenza insisted.

"It's more than that, Mother. This belongs to me. I'm creating with my own hands."

As she spoke, Doña Herminia's eyes surveyed the vast lands that surrounded Aunt Florencia's farm. They set out toward the house. Doña Herminia was working hard to try to get the part of the farm she had inherited from Aunt Florencia back into production. She had made it her permanent residence. The massive black doors of her mansion in the city where she had lived remained shut. She didn't want to return to the house that held only bad memories for her. Just like her mother, she didn't need much to live on. She was left with the property that the general had kept in her name and was not aware of the exorbitant accounts he allegedly held in foreign banks. The new government took all it claimed had been stolen from the people, including the beach palace. Doña Herminia, in her zeal to rid herself of all her memories, sold everything that in any way tied her to the general except the mansion where they had lived. During the days they had stopped speaking to each other the general had placed the mansion in his daughter's name and Sara would not hear of selling it.

CHAPTER 78

Alfonso Casals had always promised to return but never did. He had refused to attend his father's funeral because, as he wrote to his mother: "This way we're even; he never saw me and I didn't see him." Sometimes, in moments of anger he would say that he preferred to return dead than to pretend to be what he wasn't. On his dying day he had asked his lover not to accompany his body to his native country. "They've suffered enough," he said. His lover was hurt by the request but understood because Alfonso had always been a lonely warrior. He had fought for the right to be what he was, and if he didn't return it wasn't to punish his family, like many thought, but rather to spare them his presence. He returned embalmed; a red rose between the palms of his hands. And although his childhood friends and his family saw his life as wasted, those who knew him later in life saw him as an example of the best friend anyone would ever want to have. Although he never made a name for himself, his virtue and commitment to the truth influenced many who came after him and eventually became famous. "He was a poet who never wrote poetry," one of his friends said after his death. He chose to return to the family he had left behind so long ago with his eyes closed.

CHAPTER 79

Doña Herminia recognized him immediately. He was at Alfonso's funeral. She had heard that he had returned but their paths had not crossed. She supposed that the slightly overweight woman standing next to him was the woman he had married while in exile. Cousin Raquel had casually told her about it once. The black hair she remembered was now salt and pepper, but otherwise he looked the same. They eyed each other discreetly from a distance. Antonio Figueroa was waiting for the right moment to approach her. Finally, passing the casket, he crossed the room. Bypassing formalities, they hugged briefly. Due to the solemnity of the occasion, they refrained from light banter. For both, time had stood still. They treated each other like old friends united by the sorrow of the moment. He squeezed her hand lightly, comforting her for the loss of her brother. Both gazed at the deceased to reassure themselves that any display of emotion was tied to Alfonso and his demise.

"When did you get back?" Doña Herminia asked, somewhat nervously.

"About five months ago."

"Are you here for good?"

"Yes."

"How's your family?"

"Fine. I have two children...they're very good kids," he answered.

As their eyes met, they both realized that for a few seconds they were back in the past. Hermi quickly discarded any thought that was not devoted to her brother's death, while Figueroa looked around for his wife.

"How's your daughter?"

Doña Herminia shrugged, "This has been a difficult year."

Figueroa knew what she was referring to and didn't think it was the right time to discuss it. He had heard, from friends they had in common, about what had been going on in Hermi's personal life.

Before he could help it he said, "Time sure does fly!"

Doña Herminia turned her gaze from Figueroa to the deceased, but she knew well that Figueroa was referring to the two of them and not to Alfonso.

"Have your children adapted well to living here?"

"Yes, amazingly. We have always reminded them of who they are and where they are from."

Hermi smiled. He studied her closely, looking for the girl he had left behind when he went into exile. He also tried to find traces of the insanity that others had warned was still with her. She had changed a lot but still looked great to him. Figueroa was about to say something else when he saw his wife approaching. Estela wrapped her arm around Antonio's arm. Her stoutness next to her husband's slender physique always made her feel uncomfortable. Figueroa introduced her to Hermi.

"Herminia Casals. Alfonso's sister."

"Nice to meet you. Please accept my condolences for your brother's death." Estela said very formally. "Antonio always talked about him."

"Thank you. It has been a very sad and unexpected occurrence for all of us," Hermi attempted a sweet smile.

She couldn't help but think the obvious. Together they made a disparate couple. She wondered what Antonio Figueroa could possibly have seen in Estela. She was glad that Estela wasn't very attractive and couldn't, despite herself, control a feeling of triumph when she compared herself to Antonio's wife. They talked a little bit about Antonio, who was back at work as a lawyer and deeply involved in a project gathering material for a book. Doña Herminia looked at them, making a conscious effort not to look into Antonio Figueroa's eyes for fear that either Estela or he would realize what she was really thinking. Estela was curious about Hermi; as General Gutiérrez's widow she provoked a lot of interest, even from those who had lived abroad for many years. Nobody brought it up, and Hermi began to feel increasingly freed from her husband's memory. She imagined that people were also beginning to forget, but what she didn't know was that in many social circles they still pointed her out and talked about her.

CHAPTER 80

"You are a tyrant like your father!" screamed Doña Herminia in a moment of blind fury.

She could see her daughter's face, crimson with anger, hatred in her eyes. Herminia was immediately sorry for what she just said.

Sara looked at her mother coldly.

"Why did you marry him?"

"Shut up!" Herminia yelled, completely out of control.

"Why should I shut up? You're always attacking me and I have to remain silent. Where were you when they made fun of me in school for having a crazy mother? That is all I remember about you. Sitting there, not caring about anything, pretending to be crazy."

"Get out of here!" screamed Doña Herminia. "Get out! Insolent brat!"

Sara fled. Doña Herminia's entire body was shaking. She realized at that moment that General Gutiérrez would always be with her.

She sat down in a rocker and automatically rocked herself, tormented by her thoughts.

"Everything seems so far and yet so close...Tomorrow, another day we're supposed to go through in some way, and then wait for the next one and the next one and the next one, until the end...What have I done with my life? Those moments when I remained silent. Those times that I consented, thinking only of myself. When is it survival and when is it a lack of courage?

"I'm back to not wanting anything, and not wanting to do anything. What a horrible emptiness!...I've got to find an answer...But I feel that there is something mocking me...I'm deceiving myself...There really isn't an explanation..."

Lorenza was returning from examining a calf that had just been born. The far-away look on Doña Herminia's face reminded her of those times when her daughter had given up on life.

"Herminia, what's the matter?" she asked, perturbed.

"Nothing Mother," she tried to smile. The tenderness in her mother's eyes made her feel protected. "Another fight with Sara. She's insisting on returning to the city. She won't listen to anybody. Every day is worse. I don't know what to do any more!"

Lorenza didn't know either. She had hoped that it would just be a matter of time. But a long time had passed since the general's death, and Sara was behaving just as she had on the first day: rebellious and very cruel to her mother and anything that had to do with her.

"Perhaps she needs more time. She has a lot to deal with. You can understand that!"

CHAPTER 81

"Everyone is accusing me of something. 'Look at the general's daughter,' they say. Look at this and look at that...Now even my mother...What am I supposed to do? Kiss her every day? I'm not like that." It bothered her that her grandmother had come to lecture her. "I'm sick and tired of being asked to behave. I want everyone to leave me alone...My mother doesn't need me. Can't you see that? She spends all her time working."

"She deserves to be respected," Lorenza said.

"There you go accusing me, too. I know what my mother thinks. Go ask her what she said to me this morning. Who's the one being cruel here, Grandma?"

"You know she didn't mean to say that. It was a moment of desperation in response to your behavior. The two of you can't go on like this. You live as if you were enemies...Your mother is suffering a lot."

"And what about me, Grandma? I'm suffering too. Everyone looks at me. No matter what I do, I will always be perceived as General Gutiérrez's daughter. I don't want to care...I don't want to worry about anybody. That's what I want, and that's what I'm going to do."

She left the room, not wanting to hear anything else. She called her dog Wolf to her side and patted him lovingly.

Lorenza remained pensive for a while, still sitting on Sara's bed. She looked at the stuffed animals stacked in a corner. "So direct, so tough. It didn't have to be this way. Seeds from other times are germinating," she thought.

CHAPTER 82

Antonio Figueroa began to lose his concentration after seeing Doña Herminia at Alfonso's funeral. He thought that at his age he could control the impulsive nature that had gotten him into so much trouble throughout his life. But there he was, working up a strategy to find an excuse to visit Doña Herminia. He couldn't think of any. So he simply appeared at her doorstep to let her know that he was at her service should she need anything. After seeing him to the living room and asking him to sit down, Doña Herminia fled to the kitchen under the pretext of going to look for something to drink. She actually needed to get away for a moment to recover. She could feel his gaze pierce her back as she walked away. She returned with a glass of juice and a tray of fruit. She was making every effort to appear calm. They talked carefully about the past, about everyday things and about their respective plans for the future. They asked each other questions, but they didn't pay attention to the answers because between the questions and the answers they were watching each other closely. He found her to be far more attractive than she had been when he had left the country. She thought that he had not aged at all. He wanted to continue to talk about anything, just to be close to her.

"It's hard for me to call you Doña Herminia. I'd rather call you Hermi like I used to."

Doña Herminia understood his discomfort.

"I've known you since you were this tall," she raised her arm from where she was sitting to indicate an arbitrary height.

Antonio laughed out loud. He remembered that comment perfectly. Both laughed. That moment merged the past with the present. They were communicating on another level. But both understood that the past was no more than an illusion now, a distant memory that they could feel without actually touching it. He finally came up with an appropriate excuse to be able to visit her more often. He would become her legal counsel for all matters pertaining to the property that Doña Herminia wished to acquire.

CHAPTER 83

The first few visits her husband paid Doña Herminia didn't worry Estela because she knew they were old friends. She began to suspect something, though, when the visits became increasingly more frequent. She didn't think it was proper for him to visit the wife of a man that he had so deeply hated. When she broached the subject, he answered, "She was a victim, just like all of us."

"Yeah, a victim who was left with money that rightfully belongs to the people," Estela answered bitterly, resentful that her husband would defend Doña Herminia. Antonio didn't say anything.

As days went by Estela was increasingly tormented by her feelings of jealousy. She began looking for proof of guilt. She would smell Antonio's shirts, sniffing out different scents, or try to capture a change in his demeanor. But Antonio would lock all his emotions inside himself the moment he entered his house. His wife and children continued to be a priority for him. Estela didn't dare say anything, fearing her jealousy might actually turn him away. Besides, she reasoned that, if she was wrong, her suspicions might actually give him ideas that he himself had not conceived. She continued to search, however, not knowing what she would do should her suspicions be confirmed.

One afternoon back from work, Antonio found her holed up in the bedroom in the dark. She threw her arms around his neck as soon as he walked in.

"Do you still love me?" she gasped.

Antonio kissed and caressed her with a passion he had not shown in many years. He wanted to ask her why she asked him but didn't dare.

"What is worrying my little kitten today?" he asked her tenderly and sincerely. She answered by squeezing her body closer to his. He really did love her, Antonio told himself, even though she did not arouse any passion in him. No matter how long they lived together, he would never feel a need to touch her.

"Promise me."

"What?" he asked.

"That you will love me forever."

"But Estela..."

He found himself making a conscious effort to make love to her. She kissed him desperately, believing that she would be capable of anything so as not to lose him.

CHAPTER 84

"We must pray that God will allow all wandering souls to rest in peace," Lorenza prayed aloud, fingering her rosary. Every day in her prayers and petitions before the altar, she combined the ancient slaves' beliefs together with her father's religious doctrine. Concentrated as she was on her prayers, she didn't notice Herminia watching her from the door. Doña Herminia admired her mother's devotion and belief system. She had never believed in anything throughout her life. When she went to church it was only because the nuns made her. She had her daughter baptized because that was the thing to do, but she herself felt no devotion to anything. Lorenza kissed the rosary and placed it carefully upon the altar she had brought from the town of Santa María Redentora when she decided she would spend what remained of her life with her daughter.

"Have you finished?"

"Yes," she answered, happy to see her.

"Let's go for a walk."

Lorenza was ready. She could tell that Hermi wanted to talk. They walked, admiring the coffee groves, the fruit orchards, and the flowers.

"Mom, I think I finally have something." Lorenza, whose heart was thumping, waited for her daughter to finish her thought. Since Antonio Figueroa had come into her daughter's life, she had noticed a change. "All this," said Hermi spreading her arms, "so many years waiting for this. I have a place to live that is truly mine."

They passed the groundskeeper's house. His name was Lorenzo. He greeted them smiling, feeling he was the three women's protector. He had not always felt this way, particularly when he took the job pressured by need. He had scorned the city woman's pretension to run such a large farm.

He had told his wife: "That's a man's job. She's not going to last." But over time, Lorenzo became the most loyal of her workers and completely changed his mind regarding Herminia. "She runs this place better than any male boss would," he said proudly when he overhead comments made by new workers who were not used to working for a woman.

"If only he weren't married," Lorenza was thinking. "God, why have you returned him to her life? What is the meaning of all this?"

CHAPTER 85

She was waiting for her, sitting in the living room looking through old magazines. As soon as Hermi entered, she could not help but notice how much weight her cousin had gained. Her body poured itself into every nook and cranny of the velvet chair. She supposed that the change in her cousin was due to the fact that her husband had left her for another woman. Cousin Raquel exchanged a nervous smile with Hermi as she approached and hugged her. The ten years between them were very evident now. Doña Herminia looked at her warmly; they used to be so close! "There is no doubt," she thought, "everything changes over time." Raquel was happy to have an opportunity to help her again. It was like before when Hermi asked her advice about everything.

"It's so good to see you, Raquel!"
"Hermi, dear!"
"How are things going?"
"Well, I'm sure you've heard of the shameful thing my husband did. Men are idiots," she added, unable to hide the anger that surfaced each time she thought of her husband's leaving her for a younger woman.
"Oh, Raquel!"
"It's not so bad. The first months are tough; then one finds a way to keep on going. That's your only resort. Look," she said opening her eyes wide, "I really think I no longer loved him when it happened. What I can't forgive is how old and ugly he has made me feel. Men have no feelings...When they get the urge, they're gone."

Hermi smiled. She had always admired her cousin Raquel's pragmatic attitude. But she would have preferred for her to speak to her sincerely, to tell her the truth about how she felt because she knew that, even though cousin Raquel wasn't admitting it, the divorce had taken its toll.

"Let's put my problems aside. As I told you I've got plenty of room in my house for Sara. It's not a problem at all if she wants to live with us while she's at the university. You know we've always gotten along."

"I know. That's why I asked you. Sara is not easy to deal with at times."

"Well, it hasn't been easy for anybody. You know how he was with her and now all that they're saying he did. I have trouble believing it myself."

"In any event," Doña Herminia changed the subject, "I wanted her to attend the university that is half an hour from here, but she refuses and I have no way to force her because, as I told you, she doesn't pay attention to me."

"Don't worry. It's just a phase. Today's youth...Besides, poor kid! She must be quite confused."

"What hurts me most is that I know she is suffering. But she barely speaks to us..."

CHAPTER 86

"How is the city?" Mercedes asked Doctor Collado, who, after his wife's death, visited Mercedes more often.

"Like it always is. Lots of traffic, people complaining about prices and about the government not keeping its promises."

Doctor Collado felt out of control around Mercedes. At times there was the clumsiness; then he would talk too much. He had struggled with his shyness from the beginning, eventually learning to accept it. After leaving Mercedes' house he would needlessly torment himself, fantasizing that Mercedes had other lovers although he knew she didn't. He could not keep himself from thinking the worst. At times, frustrated by his own lack of initiative, he would become convinced it was true. His suffering grew as he imagined her in someone else's arms. Driven by unfounded jealousy, he would drop in on her, expecting to catch the imaginary intruder. He never found anything that would indicate there was someone else in her life.

Mercedes was eyeing him as he spoke. His eyes were tender, but the way he looked at her betrayed the same desire all men had for her body. Mercedes was holding a teddy bear Doctor Collado had given her. Mercedes could see the doctor's reflection in the little toy's eyes. She took his hands and led him to her bedroom. She took off his clothes. Doctor Collado was too stunned to speak. He was allowing this to happen as if it weren't happening to him. He simply watched as she removed, piece by piece, the immaculate suit he had worn for years.

He felt like a defenseless child. The moment seemed so simple! How many times had he imagined it! He wasn't surprised by the fact that it was all occurring differently from how he had seen it in his imagination. At his age he understood that fantasies were realized differently in real life than in dreams. Mercedes began to take off her clothes. Upon seeing her naked the doctor's pupils opened wide.

"Doctor Collado, what's the matter? Don't you want me? asked Mercedes who was in the habit of addressing him by his title. Putting his arms around her he tried to speak, but all he could muster was garbled sounds. He felt shy, like an adolescent who is making love for the first time. They remained embraced for a long time. The doctor had fantasized about this moment for so long that his excitement overwhelmed him. Whatever virility he still had left him on that very day.

CHAPTER 87

Sara lay in the grass in the shade of an orange tree. From where she was she could see the workers' children playing hide-and-seek in clothes so ragged one could see parts of their bare behinds. Christmas was around the corner, and a festive feeling filled every corner of the little town near Doña Herminia's farm. In spite of herself, Sara felt happy. This was her first weekend back at the farm since she had moved in with Cousin Raquel. She felt good lying in the grass and, even though she didn't want to admit it, she admired how her mother had been able to transform the fields into a workable farm. She heard steps behind her. Peering through her sunglasses she saw her mother approaching. Doña Herminia sat down next to her daughter and gazed out at the wide expanse of land that lay before her. From where she was Doña Herminia could not hear the tractor, but she could imagine it, and the picture gave her great pleasure. She talked to Sara about the Christmas presents she was preparing and the plans she had for the workers during the holidays. Sara felt it necessary to appear bored with the conversation. This was the only attitude she could muster in her mother's presence. Lately she had found it increasingly more difficult to maintain this attitude. Doña Herminia changed the subject.

"I'm glad that you are interested in medicine. It is a very useful career despite the fact it takes a long time...I always thought that I might like to attend the university...but my life took another path...Some of the girls I studied with at the boarding school became career women. Many of them gave it up in order to get married. In my day it wasn't often..." When she spoke with her daughter she could hear the echo of her own voice coming back to her, leaving a disconcerting emptiness. "In those days people thought that men didn't like women who knew a lot and some girls worried about becoming spinsters...Now times are changing, and that is good. I would love to have studied..."

Sara remained quiet. "Always the victim," she thought. "Always an excuse for everything. If not that she couldn't study, then it's my father. She bores me to death!"

Doña Herminia fought the exhaustion that overcame her whenever she spoke to her daughter.

"Do you get along well with Leopoldo?" Doña Herminia asked, referring to Cousin Raquel's youngest son who still lived at home.

"Of course! Why wouldn't I?"

"Does he have a girlfriend?"

"I don't snoop into other people's lives, Mom."

"He's a very handsome young man," Herminia continued, trying to ignore her daughter's brusque manner. "I can only imagine that he must have lots of girls chasing after him."

Sara didn't say anything.

CHAPTER 88

At first, encouraged by his mother, Leopoldo had tried to make friends with Sara. They knew each other from the time they were kids, but as they grew older they had become strangers. Leopoldo was three years older than Sara. He was popular with girls because of his great sense of humor. With Sara he felt constrained. Behind her back he referred to her as the Ice Princess. For her part Sara felt that her third cousin made too much of an effort to be funny. Cousin Raquel tried for a long time to get her son interested in Sara, partly because she had promised herself that she wouldn't go through what she went through with her older son Ricardo. He had a wife that Raquel found unbearable. "I'm going to select a wife for Leopoldo," she would say. Cousin Raquel saw Sara as a good possibility especially because she was part of the family. But the two cousins kept an increasing distance from each other.

"Sara thinks she's better than everyone else," Leopoldo told his mother.

"The problem is you are attracted to those foolish girls that seem to be everywhere. Sara is a serious girl who doesn't go out with just anyone."

"Oh, mother! When you decide to stick up for someone, nothing will change your mind," Leopoldo answered, exasperated.

"Poor girl. She's been through so much. You're a hard man, Leopoldo. You are not showing any sympathy here. The poor thing hasn't had a friend since she began her studies at the university."

"That's exactly what I'm trying to tell you. She doesn't allow anyone to get near her. I've introduced dozens of people to her. Who wants to be with someone who can only find fault with everybody?"

CHAPTER 89

"How's Estela?" Doña Herminia asked politely, complying with the protocol that dictated she was supposed to inquire about Antonio Figueroa's wife. She also inquired because, if Estela's name was not mentioned in their conversation, the true nature of their relationship would become more obvious. This was clear to both of them.

"Fine," he answered, equally aware of the formalities.

"And the kids?"

"Growing too fast. They think they're men. How's Sara doing at the university?"

He saw her look away as if she were hiding something.

"She's not very communicative. She always tells me that everything is going well...One can get used to anything," she added quickly, because she didn't want to elicit pity from Antonio.

"One of these days she's going to wake up," Antonio said. He was aware of the strained relationship between Hermi and her daughter even though he wasn't familiar with all the details.

Antonio opened his briefcase and took out a neatly rolled paper. He moved his wicker chair up to be closer to Hermi. Assuming a serious and formal tone of voice, he handed the document to her.

"Most distinguished Mrs. Casals. This is the deed to your property. You are now its sole owner."

Hermi's face shined with pleasure. She took the document and rolled it out carefully. Her dimples deepened. The document, signed by her sisters, gave her absolute control over the property left by Aunt Florencia to her three nieces and nephew.

"She's so pretty when she's happy," Antonio thought. He

was taking advantage of her reading to look her over at his leisure.

"You don't know how much I appreciate your help with this, Antonio."

Antonio looked at her, a sign of desperation in his eyes. He noticed a jasmine fragrance and heard the birds outside. He was having more and more difficulty maintaining a natural tone of voice. Hermi looked at him from the corner of her eye as if she knew exactly what he was thinking.

"My sisters didn't give you any problems?"

"Nobody would have offered them as much as you did."

"I'm not interested in money. The only thing I want is to be sure no one can take away what lawfully belongs to me."

"Well, Mrs. Casals, if you keep on working like you have been you're going to have the most productive farm in this area."

"You're exaggerating."

"Don't you realize how much this property has accrued in value since you began working it?"

Hermi smiled proudly.

"I really think you shouldn't work so hard," Antonio repeated.

"I'll bet you've been talking to my mother," she said, allowing herself to be carried away by a flirtation she was not used to but which helped offset the tension that would creep in between them at times.

"No, I haven't. But we should...really, I don't see the need..."

"It's not work for me. It's more than that."

He gazed at her and she knew that he was thinking about her.

"Who would have thought that you would become such a great administrator!"

"Well, I do get a little bit of help."

CHAPTER 90

After Antonio left she decided to try out her new tractor. She couldn't stop thinking of Antonio—his every word, his every gesture.

"My mother, my daughter, and my land," she would say to herself, each time Antonio Figueroa's face appeared in her mind. "There is no room for anything else in my heart. Not at my age...If one could go back, start again, erase all the memories from all those years. But what is, is. I cannot allow what I feel to ruin me...But despite everything, despite the pain I feel, have I suddenly found love? What am I to do?...Ask him not to come back?...He hasn't even said anything to me. We act like friends. Is he feeling what I'm feeling? Chances are he loves his wife a great deal. I feel so foolish when I'm with him! I'm not going to see him again. I'll make up any excuse to not see him again..."

"Poor Mom," she said to herself when she saw Lorenza appear along the way. She turned off the tractor and went to meet her.

"Oh, Herminia! Working in this sun!"

"The workers will work if they see me working as well...Look," she pointed proudly. "One more run and I will have cleared this entire terrain. It will be ready to seed soon. Has the fertilizer arrived?"

"Nothing has been delivered to the house."

"Well, what are you doing walking in this heat?"

"I worried when you didn't come for lunch."

"I haven't been very hungry lately."

Lorenza looked at her with concern. She seemed thinner. "Come sweetheart. Let's go down and rest for a while."

CHAPTER 91

The dead in the morgue were nameless bodies that no one had claimed in the public hospitals. Sara was visiting the morgue. She couldn't explain her curiosity. From the moment she entered she could smell the formaldehyde. At noon there was nobody there. She walked easily among the tables where the dead lay, looking for Felícita. Felícita was a dead woman who had recently arrived at the morgue. The students called her Felícita because among all the dead she was the only one who seemed to have died smiling. When Sara found her, she stopped and gazed at her for a long time. Felícita's skin shone with a yellow hue under the morgue lights. From the claws of death rose a serpent-like tangle of hair, stretched out like wire, fried like the rest of the body by the preserving liquids. Sara's eyes scanned the corpse. She felt sorry for Felícita, who was forever doomed to be scrutinized by medical students. She was leaving when she saw a girl approaching, skirting the corpse-laden tables. Sara pretended not to see her and quickly walked toward the exit. She was blinded by the sun's brightness. The girl followed her out.

Reaching Sara, she asked, "Don't they scare you?"

Sara shrugged.

"A medical student can't fear the dead," she said, turning her back to the girl. The girl watched Sara as she walked away.

CHAPTER 92

"I don't believe in that modern mumbo jumbo," Lorenza said at Hermi's insistence that she go see a doctor.

Lorenza's stomach had been hurting for a long time but, to avoid worrying Doña Herminia, she had never complained.

"I can cure myself with my vials," she would assure her daughter, referring to the concoctions she prepared from the plants that would cure her family back at La Costa. Lately, the vials that used to help were helping less. That was when she asked her daughter to have her old neighbor, Hemilda, come from the town of Santa María Redentora. "She's the best healer I know. She always made me feel better," she pleaded with Doña Herminia, who was chalking everything off to primitive cures. Nevertheless, to please her mother, she sent for Hemilda. As soon as she arrived Hemilda patiently sank her fingers into Lorenza's stomach. Tracing a cross she murmured secret incantations passed down in her family for generations.

"I think what's killing me is gas," Lorenza would say.

But Hemilda looked worried.

"That's not what it is, at least not anymore," she would answer, discouraged. "Maybe you should see a doctor. Those people have machines that see one's insides. I don't trust them much either. But, who knows? Some people have been cured by them."

CHAPTER 93

"Antonio Figueroa, there you are again, letting yourself be carried away by your impulses. The very same impulses that have gotten you in the biggest predicaments of your life," Antonio was telling himself, while playing catch with his son Tomás.

Antonio had struggled for years with what he considered to be his greatest defects: passion and impulsiveness. Those who knew him teased him about them, and Antonio, well aware of them, would rarely even attempt to argue in his own defense. When he saw Hermi at cousin Raquel's wedding he had decided, without applying any logic to the notion, that she was the love of his live. Destiny changed his plans when, because of his involvement in political activities, he had to flee the country in the middle of the night. By the time loneliness caught up with him he found himself standing before an altar with Estela, a cheerful girl who was also fighting military injustice from abroad. When he saw Doña Herminia again, he thought he should never have married Estela. Herminia was the woman he had always loved. Each time he said good-bye to her now he wanted to go back and tell her how much he loved her, that he would do anything for her. At first he had clearly understood why he would never be able to fulfill his dream. But, as the months went by he removed all the obstacles in his mind, one by one. The only thing that brought him back to reality was his love for his sons.

CHAPTER 94

Flanked by the two stone lions that watched over the Gutiérrez mausoleum, Sara stopped in front of the iron gate. She looked around and saw one large red rose growing to her right. Plucking it, she added it to the flower bouquet she was carrying. She entered the mausoleum and placed the fresh flowers in the vase, removing the withered ones. She sat on the floor next to the inscription of her father's name. She visited him frequently, as if he were actually buried in his tomb next to the paternal grandparents she had never met. Pensively, she drew random circles on the dusty floor with a rose stem she was still holding.

"Dad, I can no longer go on like this. I can't continue denying it. Please don't be angry with me. I love you no matter what they say. I can never stop loving you. I don't know…I feel so alone. At times I'd rather be with you, wherever you are. Then I wouldn't have to make decisions or think. I'm so confused…I want to be happy again, like I was before, when you were here."

She looked at her father's name as if she expected an answer. Then she got up.

Slowly she traced each letter with her fingers. She closed the iron gate behind her and looked inside once more. The circles of dust she had drawn were visible from outside. Her tears had distorted some of them, their perfect roundness gone.

She saw an old woman dressed in black while she waited for the light to change. The old woman wore a black scarf over her head. She was dragging a cart full of rags, bottles, and cans. As if she felt that someone was watching her, she looked in Sara's direction. Their eyes met for a few seconds. Small and frail, she had sunken cheeks and a tiny mouth. She had only one eye. She moved the other as if trying to open it.

"That old woman would give anything to have her sight back in both eyes!" Sara thought about what had just dawned on her. "Perhaps. Maybe she doesn't care. Maybe she has accepted the fact that she will have to live the rest of her life with just one." The light changed. Sara drove away, still thinking of the silent, brief exchange with the emaciated old woman.

It was nighttime when she got back to Cousin Raquel's house. She greeted her cousin, who was in the living room, and headed straight for her room. It was dark. Feeling around for the light switch she changed her mind and threw herself on her bed. The surrounding silence made her feel even sadder than she had been. The walls in the room, which had made her feel safe, were now suffocating her. She got up and turned on the light.

CHAPTER 95

Sara took a deep breath before beginning the descent down the stone steps that led to the front garden of what used to be General Gutiérrez's mansion. She walked along the front of the house and looked to her left, where she remembered a massive tree she had climbed many times as a child. Looking up she saw a black-feathered bird looking at her. They eyed each other for a few seconds, then the bird flew off to another branch shrieking: "cao,cao."

The piled-up furniture looked like deformed giants watching her from above. The further she went into the house she was born in, the tighter her chest felt. She heard a large squeal. Reclaiming the property, rats had made their home there. She walked the hallways, disoriented, but curious to see the house that she had not seen in a long time. She was deluding herself, knowing there was more to it than mere curiosity. Looking for a connection, she looked over all the objects that surrounded her one by one. She looked at the chests that had been brought from the beach palace after her father's death. Her mother had refused to open them. Prying one open, she found photographs, medals, and uniforms. Carefully, as if she might run into something ghastly, she began removing items one by one. Like a sudden breeze, a thought passed through her mind. It was a thought she had never allowed before: "Was he wearing these clothes when he ordered people to be put to death? Had he tortured them himself?" She tried to brush off those haunting thoughts and abruptly slammed the chest shut. Suddenly feeling scared, she left hastily, as if pursued by someone.

CHAPTER 96

Doctor Collado lay next to Mercedes thinking aloud, "I no longer care about anything. Once you're old you discover things. You spend you life looking and wind up with the simple things. You know, those small pleasures. I have spent my entire life worried about the future and look at me now. This is my future. You always end up in the same place. Always looking for what has been right there in front of us all along: companionship, love, that's it. It's so simple! We allow ourselves to be convinced by concepts that don't even exist, abstract principles that keep us from thinking or from changing. Fear, Mercedes. Fear of facing what one wants and who one is."

Mercedes listened to him silently. Over time she had grown accustomed to falling asleep while listening to him talk. At times she understood, and at others, when his vocabulary became complicated, she couldn't understand a thing he said. But she knew that all that talking helped him feel better about his life. Dr. Collado didn't always come to positive conclusions. His doubts would take over and then he would hound Mercedes with questions.

That night, looking at Mercedes' taut young skin, he asked her angrily, "Mercedes, how can it be that you want to be with an old man like me?"

"There you go again, Doctor. You see me as if I were all that young. I'm getting old, too, you know."

"Getting old? I'll never get to see you get old. I only have a few years left and I'm going to die without understanding you."

"Oh, oh. The doctor is being a pessimist. I don't understand what it is that you don't understand, and I don't know why everything has to have an explanation. Your questions confuse me," she said, turning her back to him.

He was hurt every time she became formal with him because he knew that this was her way of complaining to him. He put his arms around her back.

"I'm a silly old man. I shouldn't ask so many questions. Please don't be mad."

Mercedes turned to him and smiled, revealing slightly crooked teeth. She would always love him no matter how much he tormented her with his persistent questions, asking how it was possible that she could be in love with him. Those were questions she couldn't answer. He would insist that what she felt for him wasn't love but gratitude. For Mercedes it was easy to confuse the two. What she was sure of was that she missed him when he was gone, that it pleased her to see his face even though it was covered by wrinkles, and that she liked feeling his body-heat when he lay next to her, and that no man had ever treated her with so much love. She was reminded of his age only when he mentioned it.

CHAPTER 97

When Cousin Raquel learned that, for some time now, it had been rumored that there was more than a friendship between Gutiérrez's widow and attorney Figueroa, she, as always, threw herself into Hermi's defense. Anyone who dared make such statement in front of Cousin Raquel received a frank and brutally direct rebuke. She proclaimed that it wasn't anybody's business. Why would anyone dispute Cousin Raquel on a matter she so fiercely defended? Cousin Raquel had always felt it to be her personal duty to defend Doña Herminia against all innuendo, be it true or not. She alienated more than half of the family, including Hermi's sisters. She waited, as she had over the years, for Doña Herminia to seek counseling from her but Doña Herminia didn't. Stubbornly Cousin Raquel continued to defend her, and what she didn't know she made up. After arguing with Cousin Raquel, Laura, Hermi's sister, decided that she wasn't going to allow Raquel the opportunity to let Hermi know what was being said all over town with regard to her relationship with Figueroa. She made plans to visit her the very next day.

CHAPTER 98

Wearing knee-length rubber boots and tight-fitting pants, Hermi exuded self-confidence and beauty.

Laura could not help but feel admiration mixed with envy as she looked at her.

"The countryside does you well," Laura's voice rang sincere. Hermi, however, took it as one of many indirect criticisms from her older sister.

"I can't imagine any place I'd rather be. Let's go to the house," she offered while she let go the horse she had just dismounted. "You should come visit me more often. The city's sedentary life is not good for anybody."

Laura didn't acknowledge Hermi's remark; instead she complained about the overall economic situation and about her two kids who were about to enroll in the university. Then both fell silent and Hermi wondered why her sister was there.

"It's amazing how much this place has changed," said Laura, repeating what she had said on her previous visits.

"Look at this graft Antonio brought me. He says it will produce a variety of giant roses," Hermi said, pointing out the rose bushes that surrounded the house.

"That is what I wanted to talk to you about," Laura took advantage of the opportunity. "Hermi, I am your sister and anything that is said about you hurts me."

Hermi gave her a quizzical look. Laura continued, assuming a rather mysterious air, "People are gossiping about you and Antonio. They say there is more than friendship between the two of you."

"Who would think up such a lie?"

"Hermi. I'm only telling you what I hear. I, of course, denied it for your sake."

"Who's saying these things?"

"I have promised not to say who. But what I can tell you

is that Antonio's wife is a very jealous woman and can even be dangerous."

"He only comes to see me from time to time, that's it."

"You know how people are. You are a woman alone and he is a man. Who knows, maybe your workers were the ones who began spreading the rumor."

If there was anything she had protected since the general's death, it was her privacy. She had lost contact with most of the people she knew. Now it seemed that everybody was talking about her personal life.

"Don't pay any attention to it. I'm only telling you so that you know."

"Thank you Laura. I appreciate it."

Laura was satisfied with the huge favor she had done for her sister. She promised Hermi to fight any rumor she heard and to let her know if she heard anything else.

CHAPTER 99

When the moment arrived and he stood before her, all the carefully made plans and sentences devised so as not to hurt his feelings were forgotten. The emotion of having him there with her was so strong that she had trouble finding where to begin.

"People have begun to talk about us," she began, not being able to wait any longer.

Antonio understood immediately. It was to be expected. The society they lived in did not accept the notion of a platonic relationship between a man and a woman.

"What are they saying?"

"Rumors...that we're more than friends, I guess," they remained silent for a few seconds. Neither one of them knew what to say next. Doña Herminia remembered the sentences that she had rehearsed since her sister's visit. "For your family's sake and mine, I think we need to stop seeing each other...at least for a while."

"I think that's unfair," Antonio protested, not daring to look her straight in the eyes. "People are going to say what they want."

"It's easier for a man than for a woman. They blame me. Even today society gives more credit to a man...I appreciate your friendship and all that you have done for me, but...the last thing I want is for my daughter to hear rumors that I am with someone else's husband."

"Who has been spreading those rumors?" he asked, choked up.

"I don't know. But there is no doubt that they exist."

"Maybe I've been mistaken. Maybe she doesn't feel anything for me," he thought while she talked. He needed to think. The coldness in her voice confused him, and he couldn't detect feelings for him in her face nor hear them in her voice. He wanted to beg her to not break up their friendship. Trying to appear in control he said, "Whatever is right. I am here always, should you need anything."

He couldn't say anything else. Looking at her as if he were a hurt puppy, he turned and walked away. Hermi didn't add anything. She felt as if an enormous weight had been lifted as she watched him leave.

CHAPTER 100

Antonio Figueroa and his wife had been making love in the dark for some time.

Estela didn't want her husband to see the stomach that she hid behind a girdle during the day, and her fallen breasts. The jealousy and insecurity she felt grew daily. She had tried to avoid nagging Antonio so as not give him a pretext to be annoyed with her. She was no fool and could sense that there was something different about her husband even though he denied it and she had no proof. But it was enough to think that in his heart the image of another woman might exist, or to imagine him thinking of another, wishing to be with another, looking at another. It was an endless and painful torture. Of course, on the surface, everything seemed routine. Sundays were spent with the family as they had always been. Nothing gave her husband away. Estela wasn't only worried about losing her marriage. Other practical aspects bothered her as well. She had given up her own career as a lawyer to raise their two children. What would she do if he suddenly decided that he wanted to leave her? She was going to confront him about this today. She had to ask him again and read the truth in his eyes. Antonio came home at supper time, complaining he did not feel very well. They sat down to eat. The children asked him questions about his day, but his mind was elsewhere. Everything annoyed him: his wife, his house, his children. He went into his room. Estela offered to make him tea, but all he wanted was to be left alone. Estela followed him to their bedroom. She placed her hand on his forehead.

"It must be the flu!"

"I don't know. Maybe," he said, wishing she would leave.

"Did you have a bad day at work?"

"No. Everything was about the same."

"Oh."

She kissed him on the forehead.

"Call me if you need anything. I'm going to help the kids with their homework."

"That's fine. Don't worry. It really feels like it might be the flu."

He kissed her on the cheek. He was sad and depressed.

CHAPTER 101

Sara and Doña Herminia had to drag Grandmother to a specialist in the city. Lorenza suffered the humiliation of having to be naked before people who were unknown to her. Worse yet, they gave her something to drink that made her vomit, which in turn made her lose control of her bladder. Despite her strongest efforts she could not keep from urinating on herself. Humiliated, she screamed and loudly demanded that she be returned home. Doña Herminia begged her to stay a few more days until they could see the results of the x-rays. Lorenza relented, trying not to make it worse for her daughter, but when they told her that she would have to have surgery, she refused to cooperate.

"One can't hide from death. When it's your turn, it's your turn."

She asked Sara and Doña Herminia to take her back to the farm where she could die in peace.

"What do these quacks know anyway? I'm going to be fine."

And, as if to prove it, she would get up early every morning to check on the animals she had been raising on Doña Herminia's farm. She really didn't want to die because she felt that Doña Herminia and Sara needed her. Sara surprised her mother when she told her that she would be staying at the farm for the duration of Lorenza's illness. Doña Herminia was happy to have her there. She had noticed a change in her daughter's attitude which she attributed to her grandmother's illness.

CHAPTER 102

Taking care of her grandmother made Sara feel useful.

"Where is your mother, Sara dear?"

"In the kitchen I think. Do you want me to call her?"

"No. Take me for a little walk around the farm. I want to hear those squealing pigs. I used to be so irritated by the racket they made, but now I miss it. At times I can't understand myself!"

Sara smiled, because her grandmother had not lost her sense of humor despite her illness. They walked slowly. Lorenza was leaning on Sara. Her condition made her feel dizzy.

"Sweetheart, you don't know how happy it makes me to see you here with us.

They walked along for a while in silence. Doña Herminia watched them from a distance.

"I'm not going to be here much longer, Sara," she said without a trace of self-pity.

Sara wanted to tell her to not say that, but the knot in her throat kept her from uttering a word.

"Don't cry, baby. It is everybody's destiny. But I can't die leaving you and your mother alienated from each other. I don't want to die for that reason, Sara." Her eyes brimmed with tears as she looked at Sara and squeezed her arm. "You have got to get along with your mother. Make an effort. Both of you are suffering...and both of you need each other...Life has not been easy for her just as it hasn't been easy for you. Now, who is right or who is to blame doesn't matter. What is important is that we take a new path. Your indifference toward you mother is not going to get you anywhere. I had problems with my mother, too, and I missed my chance to ask for her forgiveness...She died before I could speak with her. I have carried that burden all of my life, Sara. Don't let the same thing happen to you," she paused, choked up with emotion. Sara was sobbing. "Promise me, Sara. Promise me you will try!"

Sara nodded her head.

CHAPTER 103

Antonio convinced himself that he had no right to sacrifice his sons and his wife. It was for the best, therefore, that he and Hermi ended it all. For a few days this realization made him feel better. But it did not last long. From one day to the next he found himself making plans to see her again, making up some excuse to go over to her house. His heart was confused. Desperate, he decided that she didn't feel anything for him. Why else would she have suggested that they stop seeing each other? He was tortured by his doubts, and when he couldn't stand it any longer he made up an excuse to go to her farm. Hermi was happy to see him. She missed his visits and hadn't stopped thinking about him.

They greeted each other as if they had seen each other just the day before.

"How's your mother doing?" he asked to establish from the start that his intentions were motivated by friendship.

Hermi's eyes welled up with tears.

"Not very well," she said. "It makes me so sad to see her suffer but, Antonio, she never complains. What a woman! My goodness!"

To console her with a gesture of tenderness Antonio innocently placed her hands in his. But the contact stirred whirling undercurrents of passion dormant for so long, for the sake of social protocol. No longer. Every pore of their bodies burst open, soaking every breath, catching every sound. Under the spell of ancestral reverberations they began to dance. Lost in each other, they forgot all else. Pretenses vanished. He searched for the eyes she hid. She trembled. They looked at each other. He raised her chin, never moving his eyes. He found her lips. Hermi had never been caressed by a man in love. Hungry, she let herself go.

"Oh, Antonio," she protested weakly.

He didn't allow her to speak.

"Tell me you love me, tell me you love me as much as I love you," pleaded Antonio.

Her body pressed against his.

"Antonio, we mustn't..."

"Let's not talk about it now," he said while he caressed her face. "My darling Hermi."

He held her tightly, restraining himself from giving in to his urge to kiss every part of her body.

"You don't know how many times I've imagined this moment," he whispered in her ear.

She was responding to his every touch. Their hearts joined, beating in unison. She wanted to be with him forever.

CHAPTER 104

Luisa Valverde was visiting Mercedes for the first time since she had become Doctor Armando Collado's wife. Mercedes was excited about showing her mother their house.

"You are finally a lady, Mercedes."

"I'm happy, Mom. And you should be happy for me."

"I still don't believe that you really love him. How can you feel anything for a man as old as he?"

"Mom, you're not going to change."

"He could be your father!"

"You should quit thinking the worst of everybody."

"Yes, sure. Like you. As much good as it's done you."

Mercedes looked at her. She was never going to get used to her mother's sarcasm. But at least, she wasn't bothered by her mother's words as much as she used to be. Over the years she had realized that the only way to disarm her mother was by ignoring her harsh comments.

"Come. I want to show you something. This is your room. That is, whenever you want it," Mercedes said, watching her mother's reaction closely.

"I have always told you. I prefer to stay in my own shack more than living in someone else's house."

"That's fine. I was only letting you know that this is your room, should you ever feel lonely."

"What about your husband? Do you think he could accept me here?"

"It was his idea."

"Oh, now I see. You are offering me this room because he asked you to, and not because it is something you want."

"Mother, listen to me. The room is there when you want it...Let's go see the rest of the house."

Luisa followed, muttering something that Mercedes could not make out.

CHAPTER 105

"What must he think of me? I haven't heard from him for days. He got what he was after. That's got to be it. God! He must think I'm crazy. How can I even hope to fill a space in his life? By letting him have me, I have agreed to become merely a secondary interest for him. Because of my weakness, I've lost him. He must think I'm easy. Seduced at the slightest provocation. I feel so cheap. A decent woman would have rejected him. Is he testing me? His love is a love that doesn't belong to me. Does he really love me, or am I just a distraction? Like so many others he must just be bored with his wife. Antonio. None of this makes sense...He didn't say anything when he left. He didn't make any plans, nothing. What does he want me to think regarding his true intentions for me? I'm not going to let anybody subjugate me again."

She decided to write to him because she feared she might detect a doubt in his voice if she called him. Trying to achieve the right tone, she tore up many letters. She didn't want him to think that she was asking him to leave his family. Finally she sent him a brief note.

"Some things come too late in life. Under the current circumstances it is impossible for us to be together. I beg you to forget what has happened.

                                      Forever,
                                      Hermi."

CHAPTER 106

"What do you mean, you've always loved her! What am I supposed to do? Go somewhere with the kids while you enjoy your honeymoon?" Estela wanted to wound him, to destroy him, to make him share her pain.

Antonio's emotions were overpowering him. He fought the tears welling up in his eyes. He tried to explain but was rendered speechless. He wanted to say that he had spent sleepless nights trying to suffocate his emotions, suppressing his feelings, telling himself that his actions were wrong. It hadn't worked. Without realizing it, he was walking in circles, his arms crossed behind his back. The last thing he wanted was to hurt his wife and sons. He tried to forget Hermi by not going to see her. His unhappiness had led him to make life impossible for his family. He criticized everything they did or said, and easily lost patience with his sons. The only way he could see the end to his own torment was by talking to his wife about it.

"I would have preferred not to know," Estela yelled. "You think that you have some right to have another woman. What about the years I have sacrificed for you? You coward...You are a coward like all other men."

Antonio left the house feeling both liberated and ashamed.

CHAPTER 107

She couldn't imagine life without her mother. Tears clouding her eyes, Hermi wandered aimlessly about the house. She cried as memories revisited her of times when she had rejected and felt ashamed of her mother. She cried for having come to know her so late in life. She tried not to let Lorenza see her tears because Lorenza acted as if the doctor's prognosis did not exist. "It might take one day, a month, or even up to a year," the doctor had said, who despite the years practicing medicine, could never get used to the eyes of the family members that silently begged him to lie.

Doña Herminia had grown accustomed to her presence, to her old-fashioned ways and to her ridiculously long hair. Lorenza had always remained faithful to herself. She was proud and self-confident in a way that Doña Herminia never had been. Doña Herminia felt guilty as she remembered not having welcomed her into her house, for trying to change her ways, for the years that she made her mother suffer because of her indifference. Her mother had never once reproached her, had never once asked to be treated any other way.

Doña Herminia was deep in thought when Antonio Figueroa showed up, announcing that he had left his wife.

"We have to wait. I have to look after my mother," she said, confused by the new course that her life had taken. "I can't think of anything else," she added, anguished.

"Of course, of course," Antonio said, hugging her. She rejected his embrace.

Antonio had expected a very different welcome. He had given Hermi the ultimate proof of his love for her. His heart, in love, and his tortured mind began to battle. Hermi, was determined that nothing would come between her and her mother. It was her only recourse for mitigating her guilt. To give her heart to Antonio at that moment would seem like a betrayal to her mother.

Hermi's aloofness hurt Antonio's pride. Even though he tried, he couldn't understand her insistence at keeping him away from her.

He felt lonely and afraid. He missed his sons and the routine he had established with Estela over the years. When he came to see them on a weekend and they begged him not to leave them again, he couldn't stand it. A few days later, confused, he was begging Estela for forgiveness, promising her that he would forget about Hermi. Estela, who wanted to trust in him again, believed him and accepted him into the house again with the agreement that he not see Hermi again. Antonio convinced himself once more that it was better to sacrifice his love for Hermi than to sacrifice his family. He wrote to Hermi, asking her to forgive him and telling her that he would always love her. Hermi never opened the letter.

CHAPTER 108

"I've lost him. In the end what does it matter? I'm quite used to pain. In time I'll forget him. I can't believe how much it hurts! I feel as if I'm about to go crazy. This pain is suffocating me, tormenting me. I have to wrench it from my heart. He has no clue what I'm going through. Why do I want him? He's a spineless man...I'm glad I realized it in time." she thought, while she sat with her mother, whose condition was worsening daily. Lorenza lay still, arms crossed over her stomach. Her knee-length braids on each side of her.

"Hermi," Lorenza called out quietly. "Can you raise me up a bit on these pillows?"

Hermi caressed her head after helping her get comfortable. "I shouldn't be thinking about anything else," she chided herself.

Lorenza looked at her daughter. Her crystal-clear eyes bulged from her emaciated face.

"I'm going to die before you tell me anything about Antonio," she said, as if seeing her daughter's inner torment.

Hermi was ashamed to be in love with a married man. That is why she hadn't talked about it. But she didn't want to hide anything from her mother, either.

"I don't know Mom. As I've told you, I've known him for a long time."

"Do you love him?" Lorenza interrupted.

"I can't think about that now. The only thing that worries me is you."

"The human heart is difficult to predict at times. Also, there are things that men don't see as clearly as we women do."

"I'm too old to be falling in love. Don't you think?"

"The soul is never too old for love."

"But he's a married man, as you know."

Lorenza's voice was raspy. Each word was elongated. Each syllable stretched out. The words passed through her lips as if she were speaking from a place far beyond her suffering.

"He is confused...very confused. Blinded by an array of contradictory emotions he is walking in the dark. It takes an iron will and a lot of sacrifice to discover the path that corresponds to each one of us. The tragedy of it all is that when we finally realize what the path is, it can be too late. If he returns, listen to your heart...Some changes are necessary. You shouldn't feel guilty about it."

"Mother, don't say anything more. You're getting very tired."

"Love cannot be easily wrenched out, but over time one can get over it..."

Lorenza grew quiet. She could no longer speak. Hermi held her head and kissed her. They stayed in that position for some time. Hermi could hear her difficult breathing. Her tears released the pain she felt.

CHAPTER 109

Lorenza woke up happy and asked Doña Herminia and Sara to take her out to see the hens, the baby chicks, and the goats she loved raising.

Then, her eyes bright with joy, she said, "I saw her last night, and she has revealed it all to me." Doña Herminia looked at her puzzled. "I have seen my mother and she has forgiven me." Tears of joy filling her eyes.

Doña Herminia covered her mouth to hush a desperate cry.

"Oh, Hermi, dear, don't cry for me! Finally I have found peace. And despite everything I've gone through in this life I can't complain because I have had the two of you. Take me back to bed," she requested in a self-assured and clear voice.

"Listen to me because my time has almost come."

Hermi couldn't bear to listen to her.

"For God's sake, Mother, don't say that. I don't want you to leave me."

Sara hugged her mother sobbing.

"Now I can go. They've been calling me for a while, but I didn't want to leave you. All is going to turn out well Hermi." Lorenza hesitated for a few seconds, gathering the strength she needed to speak.

"There are many things that can't be explained rationally but that can be understood by the heart. It began with my mother and the mistake she made. But this isn't the time to discuss that. That is how our paths were twisted and our destinies changed. Now I can understand many things I didn't understand before."

"Oh, Mom! We can talk later. You're exhausting yourself."

"No...there isn't time, Herminia. Now I understand the secret Frida told me."

"Frida?" Doña Herminia exclaimed. Her mother had never mentioned that name.

"In forgotten times the people of my generation believed in things that people do not believe in today. Frida was a woman with the power to communicate with the spirits...it's a long story but she was the one who asked me to tell Sara a secret before I died. Listen carefully, even though you may not believe in such things, sweetheart," she became silent as she struggled to remember Frida's exact words. Sara caressed her grandmother's arm. "They said you must break the cycle. Don't let any more children be born of loveless unions. When love comes to you don't jeopardize it for anything: neither for pity, nor for what people may say and, most importantly, don't become involved with someone just because you're lonely. That was my mistake. Love that is given as part of a compromise winds up corrupting one's soul and changing one's destiny...Here is an amulet to protect you, sent to you by people who died long ago.

Sara did not understand, but she listened attentively.

Lorenza began to cough.

"Oh God! Mother! It pains me to see you suffer."

"I'm fine and I'm happy. I have been a happy woman living with you, Herminia."

"Forgive me, mother..."

"There is nothing I need to forgive you for. No, sweetheart, what happened before was due to circumstances beyond your control...Don't feel guilty for something that was there way before your birth...You found your path, Herminia. That's what matters." She then looked at Sara again and repeated, because she wanted to be sure not to forget anything, "Sara, break the cycle. The spirits sent this message to you before you were born. They understand life and they know the secrets of death. Don't forget what we have talked about."

Her coughing became more aggravated, and she couldn't recover. Her illness had reached her lungs. She threw up, and then lay peacefully for a few moments. She grabbed her granddaughter's and daughter's hands and held them. She could see her mother waiting for her. Embraced, Sara and Doña Herminia were crying.

"Don't look back. They're going to be fine. A new cycle will begin with a different story," Rolanda Parduz said to Lorenza.

Lorenza's mother's presence seemed to envelop her. She felt the urge to look back again but she heeded her mother's advice.

Much later...

Antonio Figueroa appeared in the middle of the night, older and more haggard than Doña Herminia remembered him to be. He told her that he had made everybody unhappy. Then Hermi, who after many sleepless nights, had gotten over her love for him, felt sorry for him and allowed him to stay for one night. But the next morning she said, "Long ago we chose separate paths. I have chosen mine and I am happy... I'm not going to change it."

He looked at her, puzzled.

Looking toward the horizon, she explained, "For the first time I know who I am...

POST MORTEM

Whether truth or lie be told, doubts made up the framework of the people's collective mind. The people forever doubted the official version regarding the general's death. It was said he died incinerated in his private plane. Rumors varied. Some said he fled to a foreign country, absconding with the country's wealth. Others said they had seen him trafficking in drugs, and even others said they could hear his soul wandering about the beach palace, giving orders, pursuing those who had ransacked the palace. Years later, when a couple of aged, drunk peasants proclaimed they had been in the army and had guarded General Gutiérrez up in the mountains, the people didn't believe them. Little by little, however, the recruits' version became popular because it seemed to confirm what the people had always suspected; that no politicians were worth their time, and that the government had tricked them. According to the recruits the general had died of sheer anger upon hearing that his government had been taken over. The two friends had kept their secret out of fear. Now, old as they were, they were no longer in danger. They recounted their story in every bar they went to and whispered the secret proudly to every prostitute they slept with. Finally, the people, tired of being deceived, decided not to believe any version, and with a little imagination created their own interpretation of the facts.

Many generations later, a writer compiled all the versions in a book about popular theories regarding the general's death. This writer concluded, based on his interviews with people who preferred not to be identified, that the recruits' version was the least probable, and that there were only two ways that General Gutiérrez spent his last moments: The first was that he had been secretly executed after being captured by his enemies. The second, that he died of old age in solitary confinement, which is what a janitor from one of the state prisons claimed. According to him, he was never allowed to clean cell number ten, but he saw many important people come out of it. The official version, however, was the one that remained in the history books.

Acta est fabula.

CURBSTONE PRESS, INC.

is a non-profit publishing house dedicated to literature that reflects a commitment to social change, with an emphasis on contemporary writing from Latino, Latin American and Vietnamese cultures. Curbstone presents writers who give voice to the unheard in a language that goes beyond denunciation to celebrate, honor and teach. Curbstone builds bridges between its writers and the public – from inner-city to rural areas, colleges to community centers, children to adults. Curbstone seeks out the highest aesthetic expression of the dedication to human rights and intercultural understanding: poetry, testimonies, novels, stories, and children's books.

This mission requires more than just producing books. It requires ensuring that as many people as possible learn about these books and read them. To achieve this, a large portion of Curbstone's schedule is dedicated to arranging tours and programs for its authors, working with public school and university teachers to enrich curricula, reaching out to underserved audiences by donating books and conducting readings and community programs, and promoting discussion in the media. It is only through these combined efforts that literature can truly make a difference.

Curbstone Press, like all non-profit presses, depends on the support of individuals, foundations, and government agencies to bring you, the reader, works of literary merit and social significance which might not find a place in profit-driven publishing channels, and to bring the authors and their books into communities across the country. Our sincere thanks to the many individuals, foundations, and government agencies who have recently supported this endeavor: Connecticut Commission on the Arts, Connecticut Humanities Council, Fisher Foundation, Greater Hartford Arts Council, Hartford Courant Foundation, J. M. Kaplan Fund, Lannan Foundation, John D. and Catherine T. MacArthur Foundation, National Endowment for the Arts, Open Society Institute, Puffin Foundation, and the Woodrow Wilson National Fellowship Foundation.

Please help to support Curbstone's efforts to present the diverse voices and views that make our culture richer. Tax-deductible donations can be made by check or credit card to:
Curbstone Press, 321 Jackson Street, Willimantic, CT 06226
phone: (860) 423-5110   fax: (860) 423-9242
www.curbstone.org

IF YOU WOULD LIKE TO BE A MAJOR SPONSOR OF A CURBSTONE BOOK, PLEASE CONTACT US.